a fairy's gift

For Gregor—
and for anyone who believes in magic —K.T.

The Library of Congress has cataloged the hardcover edition of this work as follows:
Thorpe, Kiki, author. | Christy, Jana, illustrator.
A fairy's gift / written by Kiki Thorpe ; illustrated by Jana Christy.
pages cm. — (The Never Girls ; 11)
"Disney."
"A Stepping Stone Book."
Summary: When the Never Girls find out that widespread disbelief is threatening
the fairies, they have to spend their holiday break finding a way to make their families
and neighbors believe in fairies again—and save the magic of Pixie Hollow" —
Provided by publisher.
ISBN 978-0-7364-3278-8 (hardback) — ISBN 978-0-7364-8203-5 (lib. bdg.) —
ISBN 978-0-7364-3277-1 (ebook)
[1. Fairies—Fiction. 2. Magic—Fiction. 3. Friendship—Fiction.] I. Christy, Jana, illustrator.
II. Disney Enterprises (1996–). III. Title.
PZ7.T3974Fai 2015
[Fic]—dc23
2015009703

ISBN 978-0-7364-3773-8 (pbk.)

randomhousekids.com/disney
Printed in the United States of America

10 9 8 7 6 5 4 3 2 1

Disney
The NeVeR GiRls

a fairy's gift

Written by
Kiki Thorpe

Illustrated by
Jana Christy

A STEPPING STONE BOOK™
RANDOM HOUSE 🏠 NEW YORK

Never Land

Far away from the world we know, on the distant seas of dreams, lies an island called Never Land. It is a place full of magic, where mermaids sing, fairies play, and children never grow up. Adventures happen every day, and anything is possible.

There are two ways to reach Never Land. One is to find the island yourself. The other is for it to find you. Finding Never Land on your own takes a lot of luck and a pinch of fairy dust. Even then, you will only find the island if it wants to be found.

Every once in a while, Never Land drifts close to our world . . . so close a fairy's laugh slips through. And every once in an even longer while, Never Land opens its doors to a special few. Believing in magic and fairies from the bottom of your heart can make the extraordinary happen. If you suddenly hear tiny bells or feel a sea breeze where there is no sea, pay careful attention. Never Land may be close by. You could find yourself there in the blink of an eye.

One day, four special girls came to Never Land in just this way. This is their story.

Never Land

Pirate Cove

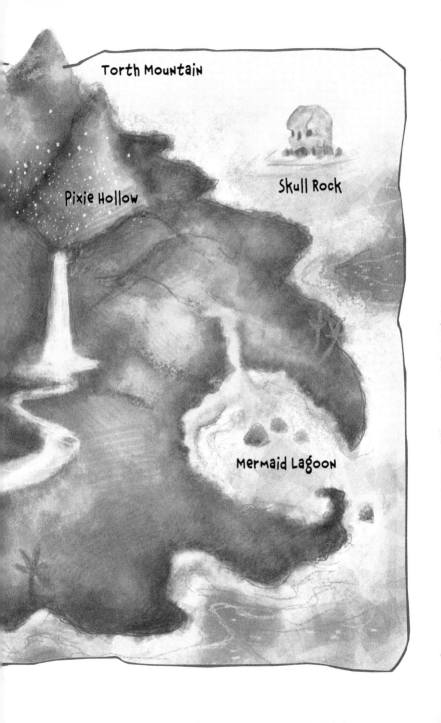

Chapter 1

Here it comes, thought Kate McCrady. Her eyes were fixed on the hands of a wall clock ticking out the minutes. Every December she waited for this moment. But this year, she felt even more excited than usual.

One more minute . . .

The school bell rang. Kate jumped up from her desk. Christmas vacation had started! Around her, other fifth graders put on their coats and backpacks, buzzing about their holiday plans. Kate had big plans, too. She locked eyes with her best friend, Mia Vasquez, and knew they were both thinking the same thing.

Never Land!

"Should we go now?" Mia whispered.

Kate nodded. "Let's get Lainey and Gabby. Come on!" She shrugged into her coat and, without bothering to zip it, hurried out the door.

In the hall, their friend Lainey Winters was waiting for them. Behind her thick glasses, her eyes were big with excitement. "I can't wait to go back," she said.

That summer, the girls had discovered a portal between their world and the magical island of Never Land. They'd made friends with the fairies who lived there, in a place called Pixie Hollow. They spent the summer visiting the fairies whenever they could, having adventures and exploring the strange, exciting island.

But ever since school had started, they'd found it harder to slip away. Kate had softball and soccer practice, Mia had ballet lessons, Lainey walked dogs in their neighborhood, and they all had chores and homework. As the days grew shorter, the time between their trips to Never Land stretched longer. Secretly, Kate worried that one day they'd go back only to find that the fairies had forgotten them.

"Why isn't Gabby here yet?" Kate asked. She didn't want to waste another moment.

They found Mia's little sister, Gabby, still in her first-grade classroom. She was sitting at her desk with her boots kicked off, drawing something on a small square of paper.

"Gabby!" Mia exclaimed. "Put your shoes on! Where's your coat? It's time to go!" She found Gabby's coat on a hook by the door and brought it to her.

"I'm almost done," Gabby said. She

finished writing something with her crayon. Then she took an envelope from her desk and slipped the paper inside.

"Gabby's been working on that for weeks," said her teacher, Ms. Jesser.

"Working on what?" Kate asked.

The teacher smiled and shrugged. "She won't say. A Christmas surprise, I guess."

Kate tapped her foot with impatience as Gabby put on her boots and slowly buttoned her coat. "Oops. I did the wrong holes," she said, starting over.

"Gabby!" Kate wailed. She thought she might burst if they didn't leave soon!

Ignoring her, Gabby carefully rebuttoned her coat. Then she put on her wool hat and mittens and picked up her envelope. "I'm ready!" she announced.

"Finally!" Kate headed for the door.

"What were you doing?" Mia asked her sister as they walked outside.

"I had to finish my Christmas cards," Gabby told her.

"Christmas cards for who?" Mia asked with a laugh.

"For the *fairies*!" Gabby exclaimed. She skipped ahead, calling, "Hurry up, slow-pokes, or we'll *never* get to Never Land!"

They ran all eight blocks to Mia and Gabby's house. Inside, they paused only to throw off their coats. Where they were going, moss grew soft beneath their feet and the air always had the silky warmth of summertime.

Four sets of feet pounded up the stairs to Gabby's room. Gabby flung open the door to her closet. The portal wasn't always in the same place, but for many months it had stayed here, behind Gabby's closet door.

As they stepped through the doorway into the darkness, the girls felt a warm breeze that smelled faintly of orange blossoms. One by one they shuffled forward, pushing past Gabby's clothes until they saw a window of light. A moment later, they stepped out into the sunshine of Never Land.

They were standing at the edge of a deep wood. A clear, shallow stream ran past, spanned by a tiny footbridge made of twigs and pebbles. Beyond the stream, up a bank dotted with wildflowers, they could see the magnificent Home Tree, the ancient maple that was the heart of Pixie Hollow.

Fairy glows danced amid its branches.

The girls sighed in unison. "We're back," Kate said.

Whenever she came to Never Land, Lainey found herself looking up at the sky. It was a remarkable color, a deep robin's-egg blue, and there was always something interesting to see. A flock of flamingos, maybe, or one of the Lost Boys flying by on his way to their hideout.

Today was no different. A swallow darted past. Lainey glimpsed a fairy with a long brown braid riding on its back.

"Fawn!" Lainey called, recognizing her animal-talent fairy friend. She thought she heard Fawn shout something in reply. But a second later, the bird disappeared into the trees.

Lainey turned to her friends. "I'm going to find Fawn and see if she wants to have a deer race. Want to come?"

Kate shook her head. "I want to go flying."

"I'm going to the meadow," said Mia.

Gabby waved her envelope. "I have to give out my cards."

Lainey nodded. "Meet you in a while." The friends always went to Never Land together—they'd made a rule never to go without one another. But once there, they often followed their own hearts' desires.

Kate headed to the mill, where she'd get a pinch of fairy dust so she could fly. Mia strolled toward the meadow, where the prettiest flowers grew. And Gabby started for the Home Tree.

Lainey crossed the stream, heading toward the trees where Fawn had disappeared. As she walked, she whistled a Christmas carol.

Deck the halls with boughs of holly . . .

Lainey stopped. Was it her imagination? Or was there an echo?

She whistled again. A throaty chirp came back, matching her note for note.

Lainey scanned the trees. Since she'd started spending time in Pixie Hollow, her eyes had become much sharper. Now she spied a plump gray bird sitting on a branch. Could that be the one chirping?

She whistled another line of

the song. The bird peered at her with beady black eyes. Then it spread its wings and flew away. Lainey sighed.

She started walking again—and the forest around her burst into birdsong. In a chorus of trills, whistles, and cheeps, dozens of birds sang the song back to her.

As suddenly as they'd begun, the birds fell silent. Lainey had the feeling they were waiting.

Heart pounding, she whistled the next part. *Fa-la-la-la-la-la-la-la-la.*

The branches above exploded into song. Lainey's heart soared. She felt like a conductor with a great feathered orchestra. Lainey and the birds finished the song together.

"Bravo!" shouted a tiny voice. Fawn darted out from her hiding place behind a branch.

Lainey laughed. "Did you tell the birds to copy me?"

"So what if I did?" Fawn said with an impish grin. "It sounded wonderful. You're a natural song leader. Can you do any others?"

"You bet I can," Lainey said. She began to whistle "Jingle Bells," and the entire bird chorus followed along.

Gabby had been all over Pixie Hollow, delivering Christmas cards to her best fairy friends. She'd left two in a robin's nest for the animal-talent fairies Fawn and Beck. She'd dropped one inside a buttercup for the garden fairy Rosetta, and another into Iridessa's favorite pool of sunlight. She left a card in the water fairy Silvermist's birch-leaf canoe. She placed one in a spiderweb hammock for Spinner, the storytelling sparrow man, and another on the knothole doorstep of Prilla, the fairy who'd first brought Gabby to Never Land. And for Dulcie, the baking-talent fairy, she placed one in an empty chestnut shell right outside the kitchen door.

Gabby had only one card left to deliver. Tucked between the roots of the Home Tree was a little building made from an old metal teapot. Gabby squatted down and tapped on the door.

She heard grumbling inside. Too late, Gabby remembered that Tinker Bell didn't like to be bothered in her workshop. She was about to leave the card on the pebble doorstep, when the door flew open. The tinkering fairy poked her tiny blond head out.

"What is it?" she asked.

"Nothing . . . I just . . . I have . . . This is for you." Gabby held out the card.

As Tink took the square of folded paper, her face softened. On the front, Gabby had drawn a snowflake in silver crayon—silver because Tink liked metal things. Inside, the card read:

TO TINK
MERRY KRISMUS
FROM GABBY

"It's a Christmas card," Gabby explained.

"So I see." Tink looked pleased. She closed the card, then opened it and read it again.

She smiled at Gabby. "No one's ever given me a card before."

"Never?" Gabby was shocked. "What about for your birthday?"

Tink laughed. The sound was clear and bright, like a tiny bell ringing. "Fairies don't have birthdays."

"But then how do you know how old you are?" Gabby asked.

"We don't get older," Tink explained. "We just . . . are. Until we aren't." She admired the card again. "I want to give you something, too."

Tink darted inside her workshop. She returned holding something shiny, which she placed in Gabby's hand. It was a silver bell about the size of a gumdrop.

"It's a fairy bell," Tink explained. "Long

ago, Clumsies hung them on their houses. It was a way of saying that they were friendly to fairies and magic."

Gabby rang the bell, which gave a high, merry jingle. She thought it sounded just like Tink's laugh.

"Of course, things have changed," Tink went on. "No one uses the bells anymore. I've kept some just because they're pretty."

Gabby rang the bell again, enjoying the sound. "It's a nice present," she said, putting it in her pocket. "Thank you very much."

"It's nothing," Tink said, waving off Gabby's thanks. "I'd better get back to work. I have an idea for a self-ladling soup pot. Haven't worked out all the kinks yet, though." She pointed to her pom-pom slippers. They were splattered with pea soup.

Tink went back into her workshop and closed the door. Before Gabby left, she peeked through the window. Tink was sitting in a chair made from a bent teaspoon. She was reading her card again.

Mia sat at the edge of the meadow, drowsing among the flowers. She knew her friends were off having adventures. *In a minute, I'll go find them,* she told herself. But the air was so soft, the flowers so bright and lovely, the little fairy doors and windows in the trees so charming, she just had to stop and soak it all in. Sometimes Pixie Hollow seemed exactly like a dream. A magnificent dream that

Mia and her friends could return to again and again.

She'd been sitting for some time when she suddenly noticed a freckle-faced fairy in a green beanie perched on a nearby daisy. "Oh, Prilla!" Mia said. "I didn't see you there. Why didn't you say something?"

"I'm just back from a blink," Prilla said. She had the dazed look she got when she blinked her eyes and went to the mainland. Prilla always visited children on her blinks. That was how she'd met Mia, Gabby, and their friends—she'd accidentally brought them back to Pixie Hollow with her.

"Why do you do that?" Mia asked. "Go on blinks, I mean."

"Because it's my talent and I love it," Prilla replied. "And because it helps all fairies."

"Helps them how?" Mia asked.

Prilla looked surprised. "Don't you know? Through belief, of course! I help children believe in magic. And in turn, children's belief is what keeps fairy magic alive." As she spoke, she drew a ring in the air, leaving a trail of sparkling fairy dust. "Like a circle, you see? Fairies call it the Ring of Belief."

Mia watched the ring of fairy dust slowly fade. She had always believed in fairies, for as long as she could remember. It had never dawned on her that her belief was important to *them*. "It must be a nice job, meeting kids all over the world," she said to Prilla.

"It is . . . usually," Prilla replied. Her brow furrowed, but she didn't say more.

Mia was about to ask what was bothering

her when she noticed a fairy coming toward them. The fairy seemed to be having trouble flying. She kept swerving to the right, as if she were being blown off course by a strong breeze.

"Are you all right?" Mia asked as the fairy wobbled past.

The fairy's glow turned pink as she blushed. "I'm fine," she said. "Think I might've strained my wing, that's all. I'm on my way to see the healers now. Just wing strain, I'm sure," she repeated, as if to herself.

As she flew off, a sharp gust of wind came up. It bent the meadow grass and sent goose bumps crawling across Mia's skin. Prilla had to cling to her daisy to keep from being blown into the air.

"That's strange. It almost never gets this

cool in Pixie Hollow," Prilla said when the gust had died down.

Suddenly, Mia felt anxious to find her friends. The drowsy, dreamy feeling she'd had a moment before was gone, replaced with a strange uneasiness.

"I'd better find Gabby and Kate and Lainey," she said, standing.

"It was good to see you," Prilla said. Her usual sweet smile had returned. "It's been too long since your last visit."

"I know," Mia said. "But it's Christmas break now. We're planning to come every day."

"Good," said Prilla. "See you again soon, then."

"Very soon," Mia promised. She waved goodbye to Prilla and hurried off to find her friends.

Chapter 2

The next day, Mia, Kate, Lainey, and Gabby sat on the floor of the Vasquezes' living room. They were trying to play a game of Go Fish, but no one could concentrate. Mia and Gabby's aunt and uncle and their favorite cousin, Angie, were arriving for the holidays that afternoon. Every time a car went by, Gabby interrupted the game by running to the window.

"It couldn't be them," Mia said when Gabby had jumped up a fourth time. "Mami said they'll be late because of the weather." But she got up and joined her sister at the window anyway. Fat snowflakes drifted down, covering the street in a soft white blanket. Mia watched another car slowly approach. It rolled past their house without stopping. She sighed and sat back down.

"When was the last time you saw Angie?" Lainey asked. She was shuffling the cards for another game.

"Almost two years ago," Mia said. Angie and her parents came for a week at Christmas. Mia looked forward to it every year. She'd been crushed when they'd canceled their trip the year before because they'd all come down with the flu.

"It's going to be so much fun to see her again," Kate said. "Remember when we built the snow fort?"

"How could I forget?" Mia said, laughing. "We couldn't figure out how to make a roof, so we used the blankets from our beds. Mami was so mad when she found them in the snow."

Kate and Lainey laughed, too. "We should

have told her it was a snow-pillow fort!" Lainey said.

"How come I don't remember that?" Gabby asked.

"Mami kept you inside because you had an earache," Mia said. "Also, it was two years ago. Maybe you were too little to remember."

"Was that the time Angie saw the fairy?" Gabby said.

"What fairy?" Kate and Lainey asked in unison.

"Oh my gosh!" Mia exclaimed. "I forgot about that!"

"Angie saw a fairy right here in this room," Mia explained. "She said it flew around and knocked an ornament off the Christmas tree. When my aunt came in, it flew out the window—that's what Angie said. But Aunt

Lara thought she made it up so she wouldn't get in trouble for breaking the ornament."

"How come you never told us that before?" Kate asked.

Mia shrugged. "It happened so long ago, I guess I forgot. Anyway, I never saw the fairy. I only heard about her from Angie."

"Angie said she had a pretty smile and a yellow glow," Gabby added.

Mia looked at her in amazement. "I can't believe you remember that. You must have been only two or three."

"Angie told me that if I always believed in fairies and kept my eyes open, I would see them," Gabby said. "And she was right!"

"Do you think the fairy could have been Prilla?" Lainey asked.

"I wonder," Mia said thoughtfully. There was something she'd been wondering about, but she'd been afraid to bring it up until now. "You guys, do you think maybe we could bring Angie with us? To Pixie Hollow, I mean?"

The other girls stared at her. They'd never taken anyone else to Never Land with them. It had always been their secret.

"Angie loves fairies," Mia went on quickly, before her friends could say no. "And she'd never tell anyone. She's good at keeping secrets."

"I think it's a great idea," Kate said.

"So do I," agreed Lainey.

"Yay!" Gabby clapped her hands. "The fairies are going to love her!"

"I knew you'd think so." Mia grinned.

"This is going to be the best Christmas ever!"

Outside, a car door slammed. Gabby leaped up and ran to the window again. "They're here!" she shouted.

The girls scrambled to their feet. Mia ran for the front door, but Gabby got there first. She threw it open, shouting, "Merry Christmas!"

"Ho, ho, ho!" Uncle Jack boomed, scooping Gabby into a bear hug. "Merry Christmas yourself!"

Aunt Lara came through the door behind him, smiling her big smile. And finally . . . was that Angie? Mia stared. The girl who stood in the doorway stamping the snow from her boots looked nothing like the cousin she remembered. Angie had always been small, with short, messy hair. But now

she was almost as tall as Aunt Lara. Snow-flakes were melting into her shiny black hair, which fell past her shoulders. She wore a trim wool coat and leather boots and . . . was that *lip gloss*?

She looks so sophisticated, Mia thought. Suddenly, she felt self-conscious standing there in her old rainbow socks with the hole in one toe.

But then Angie grinned, and her smile looked exactly the same as it always had. She threw her arms around Mia, exclaiming, "I missed you!" and Mia's self-consciousness vanished.

Angie hugged Gabby, too, admiring her costume fairy wings. "They're perfect," she said. "They look just right on you." Gabby turned pink with delight.

When Mia and Gabby's parents came into the room, there was another round of hugs.

"My gosh. Look at you, Angie. You're all grown up!" Mia's mother said.

Angie smiled and tucked a strand of long hair behind her ear. "I go by Angelica now," she replied.

Angelica! Mia thought. Even her name sounded sophisticated.

"Well, Angelica is a beautiful name. I can see why you want to use it," Mrs. Vasquez replied.

Gabby grabbed her cousin's hand and began to pull her toward the stairs. "You have to come to my room right now!" she exclaimed. "We have something to show you."

Their parents laughed. "She just got here,

Gabby," her father said. "At least give her a chance to take off her coat."

Gabby danced impatiently as Angelica removed her coat. "*Now* can she come to my room?" she asked as soon as the coat was hanging in the closet.

"All right, all right," Mr. Vasquez said. "You girls go have fun."

"Come on!" Gabby yanked Angelica upstairs. Mia, Kate, and Lainey followed on their heels.

"What do you want to show me, Gabby?" Angelica asked as they entered her room. "Is it a new toy?"

"You'll see." Gabby hurried over to the closet. But as she was about to open the door, Mia stopped her.

"Wait! Angie—I mean, *Angelica* should go

first," Mia said. It would be even better that way.

"Into the closet?" Angelica asked with a little laugh.

"You *have* to," Gabby told her. "It's the only way to get to the fairies."

Angelica sighed. "Oh, Gabby. I'm not really in the mood to play make-believe right now."

The other girls looked at each other. *Who said anything about make-believe?* Mia thought. "Just trust us," she said.

Angelica glanced from one girl to the other. "All right." She shrugged, and stepped into the closet. The others crowded in behind her—first Gabby, then Kate, followed by Lainey. Mia went in last, pulling the door closed behind her.

In the darkness, Mia smiled to herself. Any second now she'd hear her cousin's cry of surprise as she stepped out into—

"What now?" Angelica's voice was close in the dark. "What's the big surprise?"

"Ow! Gabby, you're standing on my feet!" Kate exclaimed.

"Someone's pushing!" Gabby cried back. Mia heard scuffling. The closet seemed stuffy and crowded. *Where's the breeze?* she wondered.

"Go forward!" Mia cried.

"There's nowhere to go," Angelica said. "I'm right up against the wall."

"The wall?" Mia said, confused. What was going on? Where was Never Land? She opened the closet door and they all spilled out, back into Gabby's room.

"Phew!" Angelica said as she exited, smoothing her hair. "I don't get it. Was that the game?"

Mia didn't answer. Through the open door of the closet, she could see beyond Gabby's hanging clothes to the smooth blank wall. There was no warm breeze, no window of light. The hole to Pixie Hollow was gone.

Chapter 3

"What happened?" Gabby cried. She squeezed past the others, into the closet. When she reached the wall, she gave it a hard push, half expecting it to melt away. But it remained solidly a wall.

"Something must have gone wrong. Let me try," Kate said. Gabby stepped out of the closet, and Kate went in. She opened and closed the door—once, twice, three times. But nothing happened.

"Gabby, what did you do to the closet?" Mia asked.

"Nothing!" Gabby wailed. Why did Mia always think things were her fault?

Angelica put an arm around her. "It's okay, Gabby. Isn't there some other game we can play?" She sounded very patient and grown-up, which somehow made Gabby feel even worse.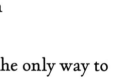

"No!" she exclaimed. "That's the only way to get there!"

"Get where?" Angelica asked, looking confused.

"To Pixie Hollow!" cried Gabby. "We went

there when Prilla blinked us, and then we found the hole and we can visit anytime we want now just by going through my closet—except today. Stupid closet!" She gave the door a kick.

"Never mind, Gabby," Mia said. "Just forget it."

Forget it? Gabby looked at her sister in surprise. Didn't Mia want to go anymore?

"We were just fooling around," Mia told Angelica. "That's all."

Now Kate and Lainey looked startled, too. Before they could say anything, though, the bedroom door opened. Gabby's mother poked her head into the room.

"Lainey, your mom's on the phone," she said. "She expected you to be home a half hour ago."

"Oops!" Lainey rushed to find her coat.

"Mia, Gabby, I need you to come set the table," said their mother. "We're having dinner soon."

"I can help, too," Angelica said, following her aunt out the door.

Mia started after her, but Kate caught her arm. "Why did you tell Angelica we were just fooling around?" she whispered. "It was *your* idea to bring her."

"But she looked at us like we were crazy," Mia replied. "And it *sounded* crazy the way Gabby was telling it."

"It did not!" Gabby said.

"Listen," Mia said. "The important thing is that we figure out what happened to the portal. Then Angelica can see Pixie Hollow for herself."

"Do you think the fairies might have closed it?" Lainey asked.

"Why would they do that?" Kate said. "We saw them yesterday. They would have said something." She chewed her lip, thinking. "Maybe it moved again."

The first time they'd discovered the portal to Never Land, it had been behind a loose fence board in Mia and Gabby's backyard. When their father fixed the fence, the portal had reappeared in Gabby's closet.

"That must be it," Mia said. "Did Papi fix something in your closet, Gabby?"

"No," said Gabby. "Nobody's been in the closet but us."

"Girls!" their mother called up the stairs.

"I'd better go," Lainey said.

Kate followed her to the door. "We're

going to figure this out tomorrow."

When the others were gone, Gabby lagged behind in her room. She had been so excited to show Angelica her special place— for Gabby often thought of Pixie Hollow as *hers,* even though it didn't really belong to any of them.

Maybe there was a mistake, Gabby thought.

Maybe if I wait long enough, the hole will come back.

She stood there for a long time, staring into the dark closet. "Hello?" she whispered. "Anyone there?" But there was no answer.

Chapter 4

Lainey stood at the kitchen window, staring out at the street. Snow had fallen all night long. It covered the roofs and sidewalks, transforming her neighborhood into a gingerbread village frosted in white.

"Ready, kiddo?" her dad asked.

Lainey turned from the window. "Ready."

"Then let's get going. That sidewalk isn't

going to shovel itself." Mr. Winters whistled as he zipped up his coat and pulled on a bright red ski hat. Lainey's dad was the only dad she knew who *liked* shoveling snow. "It's good, honest work," he always said.

Lainey wasn't as crazy about shoveling, but she enjoyed helping her dad. He sang and cracked jokes, and always made big mugs of hot chocolate with extra marshmallows when they were done.

She pulled on her mittens and her hat and followed her dad out the door. The snow had stopped falling, but heavy clouds sat low in the sky. With each step, her boots sank into the fresh new snow.

Her dad was bringing shovels out from the garage. "Looks like more snow soon," he said, eyeing the sky.

He dug in his shovel and began to whistle "Frosty the Snowman." Lainey's dad was the best whistler she knew. He could sound like three people whistling at once. As she joined in, she thought of her birdsong orchestra in Pixie Hollow. How her dad would have liked that! Sometimes, Lainey thought it was a real shame that grown-ups couldn't see fairy magic.

Out of the corner of her eye, she saw something yellow floating down from the sky. At first she thought it was a leaf, a last straggler from autumn, finally blown loose from a tree. But something about it made her look up.

Lainey stopped whistling. It wasn't a leaf. It was a *butterfly*.

The butterfly landed on her father's hat. He went right on shoveling, unaware of the insect perched on his head like a bright yellow bow. After a moment, he noticed Lainey staring.

"What's the matter?" he asked.

"There's a . . . um . . ."

Just then, the butterfly took off. It hovered for a second, a bright spot of gold against the snow. Then it fluttered around the side of the house and disappeared.

"I saw a butterfly," Lainey said.

"Really?" her dad said. "I think it's too cold out for butterflies. Maybe it was a leaf."

He went back to shoveling again, and after a moment, so did Lainey. She wondered if her eyes were playing tricks on her.

"Oh!" she gasped suddenly. Now *two blue* butterflies were sitting on the back of her dad's coat.

"Dad," Lainey began, then thought better of it. One butterfly in winter might just be a fluke. But three . . .

Three is magic, Lainey thought. *It has to be Never Land.*

She looked up and down the street. But there was nothing out of the ordinary. When she turned around again, the butterflies were gone.

Her dad suddenly stopped whistling. "I forgot the salt for the ice. Lainey, will you run around back to the shed and find the bag of rock salt?"

"Okay," Lainey said with a sigh. If Never Land was close by, she didn't want to miss any more signs. But her dad needed her help.

Behind Lainey's house was an old wooden toolshed. As she hurried toward it across the snowy yard, the wind picked up. She heard the sound of rustling leaves.

Leaves? How could she hear leaves when the trees were all bare?

Something is happening, Lainey thought. As

she reached for the latch on the toolshed, her fingertips tingled with excitement. Or was it only the cold? She opened the door—

"Ahh!" Lainey screamed. There was a storm inside the shed! Butterflies swirled through the air like snowflakes, filling the tiny room. A pink one grazed her cheek, and she jumped back, startled. Now Lainey knew for sure—Never Land was trying to reach them again.

"Lainey?" her father shouted from the front yard.

Lainey slammed the door. "Yes?"

"Is everything okay?" he asked. "I heard you scream."

"It's nothing. I just tripped, that's all," Lainey fibbed.

"Did you find the salt?" he asked.

"Nuh-uh." Lainey shook her head, leaning hard against the door. If her dad saw the butterflies—well, Lainey didn't know what he'd do. But there'd be a big commotion for sure. And Never Land might disappear again.

"I'm sure it's in there. I'll take a look." As her dad reached for the handle, Lainey wished for something—anything—to distract him.

Suddenly, as if in answer, a fat white snowflake floated down from the sky. More snowflakes followed. Lainey's dad looked up and sighed. "You know, maybe we should finish tomorrow. No use shoveling in a snowstorm," he said. "Why don't I go inside and whip up some hot chocolate for us?"

"Great!" Lainey almost shouted. "I'll be

there in a minute. I just want to . . . play in the snow a little."

"Would you put the shovels away? And don't stay out too long. It's getting cold," her dad said. He turned and went into the house.

As soon as he was gone, Lainey slipped into the toolshed. It was so warm inside that her glasses fogged over. She had to stop and clear them with her mitten. *The portal must be close by,* she thought.

The butterflies were still swirling, buoyed by a gentle breeze that was coming from—where? Lainey looked around, but all she saw were rakes, garden tools, old mud boots, and empty flowerpots.

At the back of the shed, a large bag of potting soil

leaned against the wall. A crack of light shone from behind it.

Lainey moved the bag out of the way and saw a small door. She'd never noticed it before. There was no reason for a door to be there. There was nothing behind the shed except the fence.

Lainey's hand trembled as she reached for the knob. When she opened the door, sunlight flooded in. Not pale winter light, but the warm yellow of summertime. She could see moss and smell flowers and hear the merry burble of a little stream.

Lainey felt a gentle gust behind her as the flight of butterflies shot past her. When they reached Never Land, they fanned out until they were just colorful dots against the blue sky. She longed to follow them

through the door. But she and her friends had a rule—they all went to Pixie Hollow together. Always.

She closed the door and replaced the bag of soil. She felt tingly all over. She needed to tell the other girls right away.

Lainey stepped out of the shed, remembering to latch the door behind her. Then she raced into the house to call her friends.

Chapter 5

"Just *cut* the paper, Kate. Don't rip it to shreds," her mother said.

Kate looked up from the roll of wrapping paper. "I'm *trying* to cut it," she said. "It won't hold still."

With a sigh, her mother took the scissors from her hand and sliced through the paper in a single clean line. *She makes it look so easy,*

Kate thought. She picked up a toy puzzle and began to wrap it. But the paper was too big. Kate wrapped it around twice and taped it down. The she wadded up the loose ends and stuck those down, too. She tossed the package onto a pile.

"You're not even trying," her mother said with a frown.

"Yes, I am," Kate said. "I just don't have gift-wrapping talent."

Every year, Kate's mother helped run a toy drive for their neighborhood community center. At Christmastime, dozens of toys arrived at their house to be donated. Kate liked that part. It always made her feel like one of Santa's elves, getting presents ready for kids.

It was *wrapping* the gifts that got to her. *I don't know why she bothers asking me,* Kate thought, looking from her mother's pile of neatly wrapped gifts to her own lumpy, mis-shapen ones. *No kid is going to want to get a present that looks like* that.

The phone rang, and Kate's mother got up from the table to answer it. "Oh, hi, Lainey. Yes, Kate's right here."

"Saved!" Kate cried, jumping up to take the call.

"Kate." Lainey's voice sounded breathless. "You need to come over right now."

Kate eyed the pile of unwrapped toys. "I can't. I'm helping my mom."

"Tell her it's an emergency," Lainey whispered. "It's about *you know where.*"

Never Land! Kate's heart gave a little leap. "I'll be there as soon as I can," she whispered back.

"Mom, can I please go over to Lainey's?" Kate asked, hanging up. "It's—it's really important." She decided not to say it was an emergency. That would lead to too many questions.

Her mother looked at Kate's pitiful pile of wrapped gifts and nodded. "I guess so. I can finish up on my own. Did Lainey say anything about their donation for the toy drive?"

"Nope." Kate was already stuffing her feet into her boots.

"Lainey's mother said she had something to donate, but I never received it. All the gifts are going out tomorrow. Can you bring it home with you? Otherwise, I'll have to send someone to get it."

"Sure." Kate pulled on her coat and headed for the door.

"Don't forget your mittens!" her mother called as the door slammed. But Kate was already gone.

Outside, Kate sucked in a breath of cold, fresh air. The piles of snow made the neighborhood look clean and new.

"I knew Never Land would be back," Kate said to herself. "I just knew it!" She scooped up a handful of snow and tossed it high in the air. Then she ran all the way to Lainey's house.

When she got there, she found Lainey waiting on the front steps. "Where are Mia and Gabby?" Kate asked.

"Here," Mia said, coming up behind her. She seemed out of breath. "We can't stay long. Mami said to come home soon."

"Where's Angie?" Kate asked.

"She was talking on the phone when we left," Mia said.

Kate nodded. Though she liked Mia's cousin, she was glad it was just the four of them. Something was nagging her about the day before, though she couldn't say what.

"It's probably better this way," she said. "Just until we figure out what's going on."

"Come on," said Lainey.

She led them around the house. When she opened the door of the toolshed, though, the others hesitated. Mia eyed the dusty tools and old cobwebs and wrinkled her nose. "What are we going to do in here?" she asked.

Lainey didn't answer. She went to the back of the shed and moved a bag of soil. Kate saw the thin outline of a door in the wall. "Is that . . . ?"

Lainey nodded. "The portal! But don't worry," she added quickly. "I didn't go without you guys."

She crawled through the doorway and the others followed. They came out on the mossy bank of Havendish Stream. Right away, Kate sensed something was different.

"It seems colder than usual," she said.

"What's that sound?" Gabby asked.

They all stopped to listen. Now Kate noticed a high-pitched drone, like the buzz of some irritating insect. It was coming from the direction of the Home Tree.

Quickly, she crossed Havendish Stream on the stepping-stones the fairies had placed for them. She had started up the far bank, when Mia suddenly yelled, "Watch out!"

Kate ducked as a sparrow man came hurtling through the air. He crash-landed at her feet.

Kate knelt down. "Are you all right?" she asked, reaching to help him up.

The sparrow man shrank from her hand.

"Keep away!" he shrieked.

"What's the matter?" Kate asked, startled. "I'm not going to hurt you. I'm only trying to help."

The sparrow man gave her a strange look. "You could have it, too."

"Have what?" Kate asked.

But the sparrow man didn't answer. He lurched away, zigzagging through the air.

"What was that all about?" Mia asked, coming to stand next to her.

"I have no idea," Kate said. "Let's go to the Home Tree. Someone there will tell us something."

But before they had reached the tree, they saw Prilla racing toward them. Her curls streamed out behind her as she flew. "You're back!" she exclaimed, fluttering to a stop in front of them. "We were afraid you wouldn't come again."

"Of course we came!" Mia said.

"I knew you would. At least, I hoped so," Prilla said. "But how did you get here? The portal is gone."

"No, it's not!" Kate said. "We thought so, too. But it only moved." The girls explained how they had discovered the hole to Never Land in Lainey's toolshed.

"How strange," Prilla said, frowning. "Never Land must have moved it. I wonder why. Then again, so many strange things are happening in Pixie Hollow. Come, I'll show you."

She led the way to the Home Tree. As they approached, the high-pitched whine they'd heard earlier grew louder. A fairy stood on

a toadstool in the pebble courtyard. Her mouth was open. Kate realized the awful sound was coming from her.

"What's she doing?" Gabby asked.

"Singing," said Prilla. "Or rather, *trying* to sing. Usually, she has the most beautiful voice in Pixie Hollow. But now she's stuck on one note."

"Ouch. That sound is giving me a headache," Mia said, putting her hands over her ears. The girls watched as a healing-talent fairy peered into the singer's mouth.

"Can the healer help her?" Lainey asked.

"She'll try. But there's not much she can do." Prilla lowered her voice. "It's the Disbelief."

"The *what*?" Kate asked.

"The Disbelief," Prilla whispered, as if

she was afraid to say the word aloud. "Every time a child stops believing in fairies, a fairy's magic fades. Usually, more children come along to keep the balance. But when too many children stop believing, well . . ." Prilla looked back at the poor singing fairy. "You see what happens."

The fairy had stopped her awful droning. She sat in silence, looking miserable. "I feel so bad for her," Mia said. "It must be terrible to want to sing and not be able to."

"Will she get better?" Gabby asked.

"If enough children believe, she will," Prilla said. But she sounded worried.

"Can it . . . affect fairies in other ways?" Kate asked. She told Prilla about the frightened sparrow man who'd almost run into her.

Prilla nodded. "Flying problems. Lots of fairies are having them. They say flying is often the first thing to go."

Looking around, Kate noticed for the first time that more fairies than usual were on the ground. They hopped along, flapping their wings hard but never quite rising into the air.

Near the roots of the Home Tree, several fairies were crowding into the basket of a balloon carrier, one of the fairy-dust-filled balloons that were usually used for carrying heavy objects. When the basket was full, the balloon rose into the branches of the Home Tree. One at a time, the fairies got out, going into the tiny doors that lined the branches.

"A lot of fairies can't fly high enough to reach their rooms," Prilla explained.

"They're using the balloon carrier to get to the topmost branches."

Just then, a tiny frying pan flew out the window of Tinker Bell's workshop, followed by a string of curses.

Gabby picked up the pan and was about to tap on Tink's door. But Prilla stopped her. "Better not," she said. "Tink's been in a rotten mood. None of her inventions are working."

"Poor Tink," Gabby said. She set the pan down gently on Tink's doorstep.

"I just can't believe it. We were here only two days ago, and everything seemed fine...," Kate started to say. Then she remembered that time worked differently in Never Land. Weeks could go by, when only a day had passed at home.

"I knew something was wrong," Prilla

said. "On my blinks to the mainland, it's been harder and harder to get children to notice me. But I didn't realize how quickly it would spread. The Disbelief is very catching. Queen Clarion said she hasn't seen such a bad spell in ages."

"Isn't there something we can do?" Lainey said.

"Maybe there is," Prilla replied. "I think we had better go see the queen."

Chapter 6

They found Queen Clarion in the fairy circle, the ring of mushrooms that grew in the shade of a hawthorn, not far from the Home Tree. She sat gracefully atop the largest mushroom, her long, narrow wings held high. Her glow was so bright it cast a halo of light around her. As usual, Kate found herself feeling tongue-tied in the tiny queen's presence.

A few other fairies sat around the circle, talking in quiet, concerned voices. But they turned as the girls came forward.

The queen rose and spread her arms in welcome. But her smile looked tired. "Fly with you," she said, greeting the girls in the fairy way. "We're glad to see you. But I'm afraid you've come at a sad time."

Fawn fluttered up next to her. "We were so worried about you!"

"Worried about *us*?" asked Mia. "Why?"

"When the portal closed, some fairies thought . . ." Fawn trailed off without finishing her thought.

"Why not say it, Fawn, dear?" Vidia the fast-flying fairy spoke up. "We thought you'd all gotten the Disbelief," she told the girls bluntly.

"Us?" Gabby gasped. "Never!"

"It was only a rumor," Tinker Bell chimed in quickly.

So that's why the sparrow man ran away from me, Kate thought. *He thought I had the Disbelief.* She wished she knew who had started the rumor. It seemed unfair that, on the subject of belief, the fairies didn't seem to have more faith in *them.*

"We thought maybe the girls could help," Prilla explained to the queen. "After all, they know the world of children better than any of us—even me."

The queen looked at the girls thoughtfully. "Let me ask you—*why* do children stop believing in fairies?"

The girls were silent. Kate couldn't imagine not believing in fairies. She knew her friends felt the same way.

"Because they grow up?" Mia guessed finally.

"Yes, that's true. Most grown-up Clumsies don't believe in fairies," Queen Clarion agreed. "But why? It's something I've never understood. And why do some children grow up sooner than others?"

Kate thought of her parents and the other adults she knew. She'd never thought to ask whether they believed in fairies. But it was true she couldn't imagine any of them in Pixie Hollow. They wouldn't have any idea what to do! They were always so preoccupied, so busy with their phone calls and computers and grocery lists and all their other boring grown-up things. As if those were the most important things in the world.

"Maybe . . . maybe it's not that they don't believe, exactly," Kate said, thinking it through. "It's just that they stop caring. Their minds are too full of grown-up stuff to remember about magic."

"Or maybe they give up on it," Lainey added.

Queen Clarion nodded. "I see. And perhaps some children give up on magic sooner than others."

"But if that's true, then we just need to show more kids that magic exists," Mia said.

"And we can," Kate said, with a sudden burst of inspiration. "Through the portal!"

"You mean, bring them all here?" The queen looked alarmed, and Kate saw at once how silly the idea was. She pictured hundreds of kids running around Pixie Hollow. They'd be like an army of giantss tromping on the fragile fairy world. It would never work.

"But the portal goes the other way, too," Kate said. "The fairies could use it to bring magic to our world. And we could help!"

"That's right!" Mia chimed in. "Prilla doesn't have to be the only one who visits kids."

Vidia smirked. "I'd be glad to go to the mainland and pinch a Clumsy or two. See if *that* doesn't make them believe in fairies." A few fairies laughed.

"It's a good idea, Kate," Queen Clarion said. "But it's too dangerous now, when our magic isn't strong. What would happen if a

fairy lost her ability to fly and was cornered by a cat?"

Kate knew she was thinking of Mia's cat, Bingo. He'd once escaped into Pixie Hollow and terrorized the fairies. "We could help keep cats away," she said.

"And what if the portal closed again?" the queen asked. "Fairies could be trapped on the other side." This, too, had happened. The first time the portal moved, Rosetta had been trapped on the mainland until they'd found a way through again.

"But Prilla goes to our world all the time," Kate pointed out.

"And we're lucky she does," the queen said. "But she can blink back to Pixie Hollow in an instant—the rest of us can't."

"But we have to do *something*!" Fawn cried in frustration. "We can't wait for the Disbelief to get worse." Other fairies murmured their agreement.

The queen fluttered back and forth, pacing the air. Her brow was furrowed, as if she were thinking hard about it. At last, she shook her head. "I can't allow it. It's too dangerous. We must use our magic sparingly and wait for the balance of Belief to restore itself."

"You mean, Queen, darling, we're just to wait around until our magic dries up for good?" Vidia snapped.

"We've gone through spells of Disbelief before, Vidia," the queen reminded her.

"Help!"

A panicked shout interrupted her. High in the branches of the Home Tree, the balloon carrier swayed unsteadily. A sharp twig had punctured the balloon. As a plume of fairy dust shot from the hole, the basket of fairies began to sink.

The fairies in the circle gasped. "None of them can fly. They're going to fall!" someone exclaimed.

Several fairies leaped into the air. But

they weren't strong enough to stop the plummeting basket.

Kate didn't pause to think. She raced toward the Home Tree, then dove, arms outstretched, and slid like a center fielder going for a fly ball. The basket landed in her open hands, just inches from the ground.

The dive knocked the wind out of Kate. For a moment she lay there, trying to catch her breath. The fairies in the basket looked too shocked to move. Several others who could still fly raced over to help. They took them off to the kitchen for calming cups of blackberry tea.

When they were gone, Kate stood up and brushed the dirt from her clothes. Her friends clustered around her, patting her back.

"Way to go, Kate," Lainey said.

"That was amazing!" said Mia.

Kate blew out her breath. "I guess all those softball practices weren't for nothing."

The queen flew over to her. "We're grateful, Kate," she said. "That was nearly a tragedy."

"Yes, bravo, Kate," Vidia sneered. "Let's hope you're here to catch *every* fairy who loses her magic."

"Vidia's right," Fawn said, flying up.

Everyone turned to her in surprise. Few fairies ever agreed with Vidia.

"The mainland might not be safe. But without our magic, nowhere is safe for fairies—not even Pixie Hollow," Fawn said. "Let me go through the portal."

"Queen Clarion, if you let fairies come

through the portal, I'll make sure they're okay," Lainey promised.

At last, the queen gave in. "All right. You may go—for one day," she told Fawn.

One day didn't seem like much time. But Kate thought it best not to argue.

"Fawn shouldn't go alone," said Queen Clarion. She turned to the fast-flying fairy. "Vidia, you will go, too."

Vidia's head snapped up. *"What?"*

Chapter 7

"Brrrr!" As the fairies came through the portal into Lainey's toolshed, Fawn rubbed her bare arms, shivering. "It's so cold in your world!"

Lainey looked at Fawn's thin leaf tunic and Vidia's plum petal singlet. *They'll freeze,* she thought. *Why didn't I tell them to bring warm clothes?* The fairies had been in her world less than a minute, and already she was breaking her promise to Queen Clarion.

"I might have some doll clothes they can wear," Mia said. "Should I get them?"

"That'll take too long," Lainey said. "We can find something in my house."

"You can ride in my hands to stay warm, if you want," Gabby offered.

Fawn flew into Gabby's cupped palm. But Vidia looked away with a sniff. She'd been sulking ever since they left Pixie Hollow, and Lainey could tell she thought their mission was beneath her.

Lainey's friends and the fairies followed her into her house. In the hallway cabinet, Lainey dug through a drawer of hats and mittens.

"What about this?" Mia leaned over her

shoulder and plucked up a wool glove.

"That wouldn't fit a fairy!" Gabby said, laughing.

"Yes, it would!" Mia said. "Lainey, do you need this glove?"

"No." Lainey shrugged. "It doesn't fit me anymore."

"Good." Mia ran to the kitchen and got a pair of scissors. Then she snipped the glove's middle finger to make a neck hole. She cut off the ends of the other fingers so Fawn could put her arms and legs through. Finally, she cut two slits on the back of the glove for the fairy's wings.

"Voilà!" she said when she was done. "Instant snowsuit!"

They all watched as Fawn slipped on the glove snowsuit. "Ugh," Vidia said. "I couldn't

stand wearing that. How can you even move your wings?"

Fawn fluttered her wings to show her. "I think it's cozy," she said, picking up one of the glove tips and pulling it over her head. It made a snug cap. "How do I look?"

The girls laughed. "Like a starfish with wings!" Gabby said.

"It fits you like a glove," Kate joked.

"You'll be slower than a horsefly," Vidia sniffed. "You won't catch me in one of those."

"It's very cold out," Lainey warned.

Vidia shrugged. "I'll just fly faster."

A door opened, and Lainey's mother came down the hall. Lainey shoved the drawer closed. Vidia fluttered up out of the way, but Fawn, who was standing on the edge of the drawer, toppled inside.

"Hi, girls. What are you doing?" asked Mrs. Winters.

"Just looking for some warm clothes," Lainey told her.

Her mother nodded. "You'll need them. It's cold out— Ouch!" She jumped, and rubbed her arm.

"What's the matter?" Lainey asked.

"I could swear something pinched me," her mother said. She shook her head and laughed. "I must be imagining things."

"Vidia!" Lainey snapped, when her mother had walked away. "Stop that!"

The fast-flying fairy smirked. "Just doing my part for Belief, darlings."

"We need children to believe, not grown-ups!" Mia said.

Vidia folded her arms and raised an

eyebrow. "Well, I don't see any other Clumsies around, do you?"

They heard a *tap-tap* from inside the drawer. "Oh my gosh. Fawn! I'm sorry," Lainey said, letting the fairy out.

"You didn't need to hide me. Your mother can't see us, remember?" Fawn reminded her as she fluttered out of the drawer.

"I know, I just panicked." Lainey rubbed her forehead. Taking care of fairies was harder than she'd thought!

"Vidia has a point," Kate said. "We won't do any good hanging around here. We need to find a place with a lot of kids."

"What about City Park?" Lainey suggested. The large park was only a few blocks away.

"Good idea!" Kate said. "Let's go."

As they walked, Fawn kept stopping to marvel at the winter landscape. She flew up and circled an icicle. Then she flew down to make tiny tracks in a snowdrift. "This is fun!" she exclaimed. "It hardly ever snows in Pixie Hollow."

"Watch me, Fawn!" Gabby said as they arrived at the park. She fell backward into the deep snow and made a snow angel.

Fawn copied her. "Look!" Mia pointed to the imprint of Fawn's wings in the snow. "Fawn makes perfect snow angels. And she doesn't even have to use her arms."

Vidia winced. "You'll freeze your wings. And then what good will you be to anyone?"

"Oh, Vidia." Fawn sighed and got up. She

fluttered her wings, shaking off the snow. "Have a little fun, for once."

"I mean to, darling," Vidia said. With that, she darted off so fast she was nothing but a purple streak. In a second, the girls lost sight of her.

Fawn scowled. "She doesn't care about helping. She only cares about flying fast. I *knew* she'd be useless. I can't imagine why the queen sent her. Don't worry," she added, noticing Lainey's concerned expression. "Vidia can take care of herself."

Despite the cold, the park was busy. People were jogging or walking their dogs. Little kids played in the snow. Older kids were sledding down the big hill in the middle of the park.

"Let's start with her," Mia said, pointing

to a small girl whose father was pulling her around on a sled.

"What should I do?" Fawn asked.

"When Prilla visits children, she flies up to them and says 'Clap if you believe in fairies!'" Gabby told her.

"That's easy enough," said Fawn. As the girls watched, she swooped over to the girl, hollering, "Clap if you believe in fairies!"

The girl's eyes widened. Then she burst into tears.

Fawn quickly fluttered back to Lainey and her friends. "That wasn't quite how I pictured it," she told them.

"I think the glove is the problem," Mia said.

"Yeah, you looked like you wanted to clap *her*," Kate agreed.

"Maybe we should try some bigger kids . . . ," Lainey started to say, when a snowball hit the back of her coat. She caught a glimpse of someone ducking behind a tree.

Another snowball splattered Kate's shoulder. Two boys stepped out from behind a tree, laughing. Lainey recognized them—James and Jed. They were a grade ahead of her at school.

Uh-oh, Lainey thought. She knew Kate wouldn't be able to resist a battle. Sure enough, Kate was already packing a snowball. She fired back, hitting James squarely in the chest.

Mia threw one, too, just missing Jed's head. Then Lainey and Gabby joined in. A moment later, snowballs were sailing back and forth between the boys and the girls.

Fawn tried to join in. But her pebble-sized snowballs bounced away, unnoticed. She gave up and darted through the air, calling encouragement. "Nice one, Gabby! You too, Lainey! Ooh, Kate, that's a— Oof!"

A snowball knocked the fairy clean out of the air. She landed headfirst in the snow.

"Oh my gosh! Fawn!" Mia cried.

"Whoa! Time-out!" Kate yelled to the boys. The girls ran to the spot where Fawn had fallen. Lainey gently plucked her from the snow and set her upright.

"Are you okay?" she asked, brushing the fairy off with her mitten.

"I think so," Fawn said, though she looked a bit stunned.

Another round of snowballs pelted the girls' backs. Kate spun around, furious.

"I said *time-out*!" she yelled at the boys.

"What for?" James asked.

"Our fairy got hit!" Gabby told them.

The boys looked at each other and snickered. "Yeah, right," Jed said, rolling his eyes. "That's a good one."

"You're just stalling," James said. He picked up another handful of snow.

"They can't see Fawn," Mia whispered. "I don't think they believe in fairies."

"A time-out is a time-out, all the same," Kate said. She began to stomp toward the boys. "Hey, weren't you listening? I said—"

At that moment, Jed let the snowball fly. They could all see it was a perfect throw—the ball headed right for Kate's forehead. Kate only had time to squeeze her eyes shut—

Pfff! The snowball suddenly exploded in midair, inches from Kate's nose.

"What the—?" Jed looked startled.

Kate opened her eyes. She looked surprised, too.

Vidia was hovering in the air beside her. The fast-flying fairy shook snow from her wings. Her pale, thin face wore a satisfied smile.

But the boys couldn't see her. James threw another snowball. Vidia flew straight at it as it sailed through the air. When she hit it, the snowball smashed into bits.

"What on earth?" James muttered. The boys began to throw more snowballs, faster and faster. Vidia flew to meet each one, so fast she was only a blur in the air. Her glow blazed brightly.

No wonder Queen Clarion sent her, Lainey thought. Vidia could sometimes be a pain. But she was the strongest, fastest fairy in all of Pixie Hollow, and she wasn't afraid of anything.

Finally, the boys gave up, looking impressed. "How did you *do* that?" Jed asked the girls.

The friends glanced at each other and

laughed. "Don't mess with us," Mia warned him.

"Yeah!" Gabby cried. "*We've* got fairy magic!"

"Come on, guys. We have fairies to help," Kate said. The girls linked arms and walked away, with Fawn and Vidia flying among them.

"If they didn't believe in fairies before, they sure do now," Lainey said, giggling. "Vidia, that was really cool."

Vidia shrugged. But she accepted the tissue that Lainey held out to her, wrapping it around her shoulders like a blanket. Lainey could tell she was pleased.

"Maybe Fawn and Vidia should burst snowballs for *everyone* in the park," Kate said. "What do you say, Fawn?"

Fawn didn't answer. She seemed to be struggling to fly. Without warning, the animal-talent fairy fell from the air.

"Oh no!" Lainey cried, hurrying to pick her up. "Is it the Disbelief?" she asked, cradling the fairy in her mittens.

"I don't think so," Fawn said. "I think my wings are too cold. If they freeze, they could be ruined." Lainey could see icy crystals forming on Fawn's wings.

"I told you not to go rolling around in the snow," Vidia said.

"We'll take you back to Pixie Hollow," Lainey told Fawn. "The healing-talent fairies will know what to do."

"But our plans . . . ," Fawn protested.

Lainey's mind was made up. "I told Queen Clarion I wouldn't let anything happen to you."

"Oh no!" Mia said suddenly, clapping her hand over her mouth. "I forgot! I promised Mami we'd be home ages ago!"

"You and Gabby go home, then," Kate said. "Lainey and I can take Fawn to the portal, and Vidia can help her from there."

But just as they reached the edge of the park, Vidia shot away again without a word. "Vidia, come back!" Lainey cried.

"Where did she go?" Kate asked. They scanned the park, but all they saw was a boy walking a dog.

"Maybe she wanted to fly around the park again," Fawn said.

"Ugh, Vidia. Just when you think she's okay, she does something selfish," Kate complained.

"Should we leave without her?" Lainey wondered.

Suddenly, the boy with the dog gave a loud yelp. He stopped abruptly, yanking the leash so hard that the dog yelped, too. The boy rubbed his face as though he'd been stung.

Vidia returned a moment later, grinning. "Where did you go?" Lainey asked.

"Just doing my duty, dear one. Helping Clumsies to believe," she said. And she gave Lainey's cheek a hard pinch to show what she meant.

Chapter 8

As Mia and Gabby returned home from the park, stamping the snow from their boots, they heard their mother calling. "Mia, Gabby, come in here, please."

"Coming, Mami!" Mia yelled. She could tell by their mother's voice that they were in trouble. The sisters quickly looked each other over. When they returned from their trips to Pixie Hollow, they were always careful to brush the fairy dust off their clothes and comb the petals from their hair.

When she was sure there was no trace of Never Land on them, Mia took a deep breath and walked into the kitchen, with Gabby trailing behind her.

Their mother was sitting alone at the table, addressing Christmas cards. "Where is everybody?" Mia asked.

"Papi took Aunt Lara and Uncle Jack to visit some old friends. Angelica is upstairs." Her mother put down her pen and gave them a stern look. "Where have you been, Mia? I expected you home over an hour ago. I called Lainey's house. Her mother said you'd gone to the park."

Mia nodded. "I'm sorry Mami, I forgot

to tell you. Something came up—"

"Something *important*," Gabby chimed in.

Mia gave her a sharp look. "And we just lost track of the time," she finished, before her little sister could start talking about Never Land.

"I always need to know where you are. You know that," their mother said. "But that's not the only thing. You don't get to see Angelica and Aunt Lara and Uncle Jack very often. I know how much you were looking forward to their visit. Mia, I don't want you running off with your friends the whole time your cousin is here."

"We won't," Mia promised. "It was just this once."

"Good," her mother said, nodding. "Angelica's up in your room. She's probably bored.

I'm sure she'll be glad you're back."

As the girls headed upstairs, Gabby whispered, "Are we going to tell Angie about the fairies?"

Mia nodded. "She always has really good ideas. I bet she'll know how to help."

Angelica was lying on Mia's bed, listening to music. Several pieces of colored string were laid out beside her, and she was twisting them into a complicated braid. When she saw Mia and Gabby, she sat up and took off her headphones. "Hey, guys! Did you have fun at Lainey's?" she asked.

"We went to Pixie Hollow," Gabby said, jumping up on the bed next to her. "But it's really sad. The fairies don't have enough magic because kids don't believe."

"Gosh, that does sound sad. I hope they'll

be okay," Angelica said. She winked at Mia.

Suddenly, Mia had an uneasy feeling. Something had been nagging at her all morning while they were in Pixie Hollow. She realized now what it was.

Mia sat down next to her cousin on the bed. "Ang, do you remember when you saw a fairy?" she asked.

"You mean, that time I broke the Christmas ornament?" Angelica said.

"*You* didn't break it," Gabby reminded her. "The fairy did. She knocked it off the tree. Don't you remember?"

"Oh, Gabby, you didn't really think that old story was true, did you?" Angelica asked.

Gabby looked startled. But only for a second. "It could have been Prilla you saw, because she visits kids all over the world,"

she said. "Maybe you *did* see her and that's what gave you the idea to say a fairy broke the ornament."

Angelica smiled. She leaned over and kissed Gabby on the forehead. "Gabs, that's what I love about you. You have a beautiful imagination and you never give up hope."

Gabby beamed, clearly pleased. But Mia's nagging feeling grew stronger. Was it possible . . . that their cousin *didn't* believe in fairies? Maybe she had never believed at all.

No way! Mia argued with herself. *Not Angie. She loves fairies!*

Gabby didn't seem to notice that anything was wrong. She leaned over, examining the braided strings. "What are you making?"

"A friendship bracelet," Angelica said. She held up the half-finished braid to show them.

"It's pretty," Mia said, relieved to change the subject. Angelica had used several different shades of blue string. Twisted together, they reminded Mia of the ocean around Never Land.

"My friends make even better ones."

Angelica pulled back her sleeve to reveal a stack of colorful bracelets.

"Wow! You have a lot of friends!" Gabby said.

"This one's from Lily." Angelica pointed to one of the bracelets. "She's my best friend on the volleyball team. And these are from Chloe and Clarissa—we're in choir together. And this one's from Jules. We're going to start a fashion blog someday—"

"A fashion blog?" Mia asked.

"When I get older I'm going to be a fashion blogger," Angelica told her. "Or a heart surgeon. I haven't decided which yet."

"Wow." Mia hadn't known her cousin cared that much about fashion—or hearts. "Do you have bracelets from all your friends?"

"Most of them. We all gave each other

friendship bracelets for Christmas."

"Oh," Mia said. She planned to give Angelica a book of fairy tales for Christmas. But suddenly her gift seemed silly and baby-ish. A handmade bracelet was much cooler.

"Want me to show you how to make them?" Angelica asked.

Mia and Gabby both nod-ded.

Angelica took several colored strings from a plastic bag. She taped the ends to a book, then showed the girls how to weave them in a pattern.

"I can't do it," Gabby complained after a minute. "It keeps getting tangled." She threw the strings down. "Can we play Cupcake Adventure instead?" Cupcake Adventure was Gabby's favorite board game.

Mia rolled her eyes. "That game is for little kids. Angelica doesn't want to play that."

"I don't mind," Angelica said.

"I'll get it!" cried Gabby as she ran to find the game. Mia kept working on her bracelet.

"You're really good at this," Angelica said, watching her. "It took me a lot longer to get the hang of it."

It's like making flower chains with the garden fairies, Mia thought. But she didn't feel like saying it to Angelica.

"Why don't we go shopping tomorrow?" Angelica suggested. "We'll pick out string in the colors you like. We could go downtown and look in some stores and have lunch. You think your mom would let you?"

"Yes!" Mia had never been shopping

without her parents. But she loved the idea of spending a whole afternoon with her cousin. Mia was sure her mom would say yes.

Gabby came running back with the board game. As they sat down to play, Mia thought, *Tomorrow we'll have the whole day to talk. Angie will remember how much she loves fairies, and then we can all go to Pixie Hollow together.*

Feeling better, Mia picked up the dice and rolled her turn.

Chapter 9

After breakfast the next morning, Gabby stood by the door. She watched as Mia buttoned her coat. "Why can't I go, too?" she asked.

"I told you," Mia said. "We're going shopping. You wouldn't have fun."

"It *sounds* fun," Gabby grumbled. She didn't understand why she hadn't been invited to go along with Mia and Angelica. Even her mother had sided with Mia this time.

"We'll play Cupcake Adventure again when we get back. Okay, Gabby?" Angelica promised as they headed out the door.

Gabby watched from the window as the older girls walked to the bus stop. There was a lumpy feeling in her chest, like the time she'd swallowed a gummy bear and it had gotten stuck halfway down. She'd imagined all the fun things they would do now that Gabby was finally big enough to play with Mia and Angie. Only it seemed as if the game kept changing. It was as if the older girls kept running ahead of her and she couldn't keep up.

"But *you'll* play with me. Won't you, Bingo?" Gabby said to their cat, who was dozing on the couch. She scooped him up and nuzzled his head.

Bingo meowed in protest. He twisted free from her arms and stalked off to find another patch of sunshine.

Gabby sighed and shoved her hands into her sweater pockets. She felt something round and hard. When she pulled it out, she saw that it was the bell Tinker Bell had given her.

Gabby remembered what Tink had told her about Clumsies hanging the bells up to welcome fairies. She put the bell back in her pocket, found her coat, and went outside.

The wind was blowing hard as Gabby looked around for a place to hang the bell. At the edge of the yard, there was a small, bare tree. By standing on her tiptoes, she could just reach the lowest branch. There was a bit of thread tied at the top of the bell. Gabby looped it over the end of the branch, then stood back to admire it.

The bell jingled in the wind. Gabby smiled. It was the sound of a fairy, the sound of Pixie Hollow. *But there should be more of them,* she thought.

She went back inside. In the kitchen, she found her mother drinking tea with Aunt Lara. "Do we have any bells that I can use?" Gabby asked her.

"What kind of bells?" her mother said.

"Little ones that make a jingly sound," said Gabby.

"Check the craft bin. And there's a box of Christmas decorations in the hallway. You could look there, too."

The craft bin offered nothing. But in the Christmas box, Gabby found a long garland hung with gumdrop-shaped bells. She grabbed a pair of scissors from the bin. Then she went to the phone and dialed Lainey's number.

"I was just about to call you guys," Lainey said when she picked up. "Tell Mia to come over. Kate said she'd be here soon."

"Mia isn't here," Gabby said. "She went shopping with Angelica."

"Shopping?" Lainey sounded surprised. "I thought we were going to Pixie Hollow. Did she forget?"

"I don't know. Can you come get me?" Gabby asked. "I'm not allowed to walk by myself."

"All right," Lainey said with a sigh. "I'll be right over."

When Lainey arrived, Gabby was waiting for her on the top step. She had the bells, the scissors, and a roll of thin gift-wrap ribbon.

"I can't believe Mia left," Lainey complained as she came up. "Did she forget that the fairies need our help?"

"I don't know." Gabby snipped one of the

bells off the garland. Then she cut a piece of string from the roll and carefully threaded it through the loop at the top of the bell. "Can you tie this to that tree?" she asked Lainey. "I'm not so good at bows yet."

Lainey took the bell and tied it to a branch. When she was done, Gabby handed her another bell to hang.

"Why are we doing this?" Lainey asked as she tied a knot and looped it over a branch.

Gabby explained what Tink had told her about the bells welcoming fairies.

"But there aren't any fairies here to hear them," Lainey pointed out.

"Maybe there are. You never know," said Gabby. With sudden inspiration, she added, "But even if there aren't, people will *think* there are fairies. They'll hear the bells ringing and they'll think it's magic."

"No they won't," said Lainey. "They'll think it's bells."

Gabby considered this. "Then we'll hide them," she decided. "So it'll be *mysterious*."

"I guess it's worth a shot." Lainey pointed up the street. "Let's tie some on that tree over there."

They worked their way up the block, tying the bells on tree branches, bushes, and garden gates. Gabby lost count after twenty-three. When the wind blew, the bells jingled in a pleasing way.

"It *does* sound like fairies," Lainey admitted.

They'd just finished tying a bell to a fence post when they saw Kate running up the street. She was waving a piece of paper.

"I've been thinking up ways to stop the Disbelief," Kate said as she joined them. "I've got some really good ideas. What are you doing with all those bells?"

"It's Gabby's idea. Tell her, Gabby," Lainey said.

Gabby explained, feeling proud that she'd come up with it all by herself. But Kate just laughed. "That won't work, Gabby. It's not even real magic."

"Somebody might believe it is," Gabby said. "And believing is how magic begins."

"We need to do something *big* to get people to notice," Kate said. "First thing today, we'll ask Queen Clarion for some fairy dust and—"

Lainey cut her off. "We can't go to Pixie Hollow until Mia gets back."

"Where *is* Mia?" Kate asked, looking around.

"She went shopping with Angelica. Nobody else was invited," Gabby informed her.

"Shopping?" Kate wrinkled her nose. "How is *that* going to help the fairies?"

Gabby shrugged. Somehow it made her feel better that Kate was annoyed at Mia, too.

"What should we do?" Lainey asked.

Kate chewed her lip, thinking. "I think we should go anyway . . . without Mia," she said at last.

"What about our rule to always go to Never Land together?" Lainey said.

"We made the rule. We can break it," Kate replied. "We can't wait around all day for Mia. The fairies need our help now. Come on." Without waiting for an answer, she stomped down the street to Lainey's house.

But when they got to the toolshed, Lainey hesitated. "What if Mia finds out we left her behind?"

"Well, she left *us* behind, didn't she?" Kate argued. "Besides, what's more important—our rule, or helping the fairies?" She flipped the latch.

As she opened the door, Kate flung up her hands. She fell backward in the snow as a dazzle of colored light poured from the shed. Two fairies raced out through the open door. It was the water fairy Silvermist and her friend Iridessa, a light talent.

"Quick!" Iridessa shouted. "Shut the door! Hurry!"

Chapter 10

Before Kate could think what to do, Lainey lunged forward and slammed the toolshed door. At once, the light disappeared.

"What happened? Are you all right?" she asked as Kate picked herself up from the snow.

Kate nodded, though stars still danced before her eyes from the bright light. "What *was* that?" she asked the fairies.

"Did something follow you from Never Land?" Gabby whispered.

The fairies laughed. Now that the door was closed, they seemed to relax. "In a way," Silvermist said. "Fawn told us about your snowballs. I think it might have helped. Yesterday, two fairies got their flight back."

"Really?" Kate was pleased. They hadn't heard any news from Pixie Hollow since they'd sent Fawn through the portal the day before.

Iridessa nodded. "But there's so much more to do. We want to help, too. We brought some magic of our own."

Real fairy magic? That's just what we need. Kate reached for the handle to the shed door again.

"Don't open it all the way," Iridessa

warned her. "And be careful. It's very—"

Kate shielded her eyes as she opened the door and blinding light spilled out.

"Bright," Iridessa finished.

Bands of misty light filled the shed, coloring everything.

"It's a *rainbow*," Gabby whispered.

"Iridessa and I made it together," Silvermist told them.

Kate stuck her hand into the shed. Her fingers passed right through the light and lit up blue. The rainbow rippled like water where she touched it. "Wow," she gasped.

"What are we supposed to do with it?" Lainey asked.

The fairies glanced at each other. "Er, we were hoping *you'd* figure that part out," Iridessa said.

Even though Kate was holding the door tight, the rainbow seemed to be pushing against it. She shoved the door closed and flipped the latch to lock it. "It's perfect," she declared, turning to her friends. "It's exactly what we need."

"It is?" asked Lainey.

"Yes," Kate said. "Think about it. What would you do if you saw a rainbow on your street?"

"I'd follow it to the end and find the pot of gold," Gabby said.

"Right," said Kate. "Only with this rainbow, you'll find fairies. See? That's what we've been doing wrong. We're going to one kid at a time to make them believe. But every kid in the city will see this rainbow—they'll come to *us*!"

"Every kid in the city will come here?" Lainey glanced at the shed door. It was straining on its hinges. "I don't think my parents will like that."

Suddenly, the latch on the toolshed gave way. The door burst open and colored light poured out. The rainbow shot across the yard, bounced off the side of Lainey's house, and arced up toward the sky.

"Quick, before it flies away!" Iridessa yelled.

The girls and the fairies chased after the rainbow. Kate reached it first. But when she tried to grab the end, her hand passed right through it!

The fairies zoomed past her. They caught up with the rainbow at the edge of Lainey's yard. The fairies hands could grip it tightly.

"How do you do that?" Kate asked. In the fairies' hands, the rainbow seemed soft and supple, like silk.

"We have the magic touch," Iridessa said. She was fluttering her wings hard to keep the rainbow from flying away. "Though maybe we shouldn't have made it quite so big," she added. Stretched out to its full length, the rainbow reached higher than the tallest building in their neighborhood. It flapped in the wind like a giant scarf.

"Have you got something we can put it in? Until we decide what to do?" Silvermist asked.

"I don't think it would even fit inside my whole house," Lainey said.

"They fold up nicely," Silvermist assured her. "Just find something we can close tight."

Lainey ran into her house. She returned moments later with a large cardboard box. "It was the biggest thing I could find," she said.

The girls watched as the fairies yanked, pulled, and stuffed the rainbow into the box. Bit by bit, the rainbow grew shorter, until it was just a square of colored light, so bright it hurt Kate's eyes to look at. When the rainbow was all inside, Lainey quickly closed the flaps and taped the box up tight. But light still streamed from the cracks.

"My parents are going to notice that," she said.

"Why don't you wrap it up like a present?" Gabby suggested.

"Good idea, Gabby!" Kate said.

Lainey went inside again, and returned with scissors, tape, and a roll of wrapping paper. Kate knelt on the floor of the shed and quickly wrapped the box. Since she wasn't very good at wrapping, she had to use a lot of tape. But it worked. When she was done, not even a faint glow showed through.

"It doesn't look very nice," said Gabby, eyeing the rumpled package.

"It doesn't have to look nice," Kate huffed. "It just has to hold for a little bit." She lifted the box and was surprised at how light it was. The box felt empty!

"We could take it back to the park," Lainey suggested. "There will be lots of people there."

"I was thinking we should go downtown," Kate said. "There will be even more people there." *And won't Mia feel sorry when she sees what she's missed,* she thought.

The back door to Lainey's house opened. Her dad stuck his head out. "Time to eat! Gabby, Kate, can you stay for lunch?" he asked, looking right past the fairies.

"Dad," Lainey said. "We're kind of busy."

"Not too busy to eat," her dad said. "And you need to come warm up. I can see Gabby shivering."

Gabby wasn't the only one. All the girls were shivering. And though the fairies had dressed in caterpillar-wool sweaters and pussy-willow earmuffs, they looked cold, too.

"I'm hungry," Gabby whispered.

"Me too," Kate admitted.

"Good. Sandwiches and hot chocolate

coming up," said Lainey's dad, heading back inside.

"Come on," Lainey whispered to the fairies. "My dad makes great hot chocolate. You can have some, too."

Kate was still holding the boxed-up rainbow as they trooped inside. She set the box down in the hallway, then followed her friends into the kitchen. At the table, Lainey's father handed around steaming mugs of hot chocolate and plates of sandwiches. Kate wrapped her cold fingers around the warm mug gratefully.

The doorbell rang. When her dad left to answer it, Lainey poured a bit of hot

chocolate into the cap from a tube of lip balm. She passed it to the fairies.

Silvermist took a tiny sip. "Mmm," she said.

Iridessa pointed at the melting white blob inside Kate's cup. "What's that?"

"Don't tell me you've never seen a marshmallow?" Kate said.

Lainey took two big marshmallows from

the bag on the counter. She placed one in front of each fairy. "*That's* a marshmallow."

Silvermist carefully sat down on hers. "Very comfortable," she declared.

The girls giggled. "You're supposed to *eat* it!" Gabby told her.

Iridessa picked up her marshmallow and nibbled it. "It's like eating a pillow," she said, making a face. "A *sticky* pillow."

"Exactly! That's what makes them so good." Kate took another marshmallow from the bag and popped it in her mouth.

"Lainey!" her dad called from the other room. "There's someone here from the community center. Do you know anything about a toy donation?"

"Oh!" Kate slapped her forehead. "My mom said someone was coming today to pick up your family's donation. I was supposed to tell you yesterday, but I forgot."

"Did you check by the door?" Lainey called to her dad. "Mom might have left it there."

They heard him shuffling around. "Here it is," he said to the person at the door. A moment later, they heard the door close.

Mr. Winters returned to the kitchen. "You all look much better," he said. "You see what a little hot chocolate can do?"

Kate drained the rest of her mug and stood up. "Thanks, Mr. Winters."

The other girls got up, too, and put on their coats. In the hallway, though, Kate stopped. "Where's the box?" she said.

"What do you mean?" Lainey asked.

"The box with the rainbow," Kate

whispered. "I left it right here." She pointed to the empty spot.

"Dad," Lainey called, her voice quavering a little. "What did you give the person at the door?"

"That big box in the hallway," he called back. "Why?"

"Oh no!" Kate whispered. "He gave away the rainbow!"

Chapter 11

Downtown, Mia and Angelica weaved through crowded sidewalks on their way to the bead store. People hurried past, their arms loaded with shopping bags. Everyone seemed happy and excited.

"Look!" Angelica stopped in front of a department store window. Mannequins in fancy dresses stood among golden reindeer. Their hands rested lightly on the deers' heads. Mia thought of Lainey and the deer she liked to ride in Pixie Hollow.

"Which one would you choose?" Angelica asked.

"That one," Mia said. She pointed to a reindeer that seemed to be nuzzling the mannequin's hand. "He looks friendly."

Angelica giggled. "I meant, which *dress* would you choose, silly."

"Oh!" Mia laughed at herself and studied the gowns. They looked expensive, in rich, dark-colored fabrics—burgundy, gold, and black. They seemed meant to be worn at midnight balls. "I like the gold one," she said.

"Nice! I pick that one." Angelica pointed to a dress made of burgundy lace. Mia

imagined the two of them heading off to a grand event together in their elegant new dresses.

The bead store was just around the corner. "Wow!" Mia said as they walked inside. The tiny shop was crammed with trays full of beads, stones, polished rocks, and metal charms. "It's like walking into a treasure chest!"

"Can I help you?" asked a woman behind the counter.

When Angelica explained that they were looking for thread for friendship bracelets, the woman led them over to a corner of the store. Packets of thread in every color hung on the wall.

"You'll want at least three colors for one bracelet," Angelica told Mia. "But I'd get more if I were you. Then you can mix them up and do different kinds of patterns."

Mia spent a long time looking at the colors. There were so many to choose from! At last she chose a blue that was the exact shade of the sky over Pixie Hollow. She also picked a deep green that reminded her of the moss on the shores of Havendish Stream. She picked soft pink and bright yellow and lavender, the colors of the flowers that grew in the meadow. Finally, she chose a pretty teal, like the waves that broke on Never Land's shore. She carried the packets of thread up to the counter.

"I like your earrings," Angelica said to the young woman who rang them up. The earrings were made from little clusters of purple beads.

"They were easy to make. I can show you where to find the beads, if you want," the saleswoman said.

"They would look good on you, Mia," Angelica said.

Mia shrugged. "They're pretty. But I don't have pierced ears."

"You don't?" Angelica checked Mia's ears, as if she couldn't believe it. "Why not? Won't your parents let you?"

"Mami always said I could get them pierced whenever I want. I just never did. I'm afraid it will hurt," Mia admitted.

"Only for a second," Angelica told her. "We should do it today!"

"Today?" Mia gulped.

"Why not? *All* the girls in middle school have their ears pierced," Angelica said.

"There's a jewelry store down the street," the woman told them. "I think they pierce ears there."

As they walked to the jewelry store, Mia's stomach felt fluttery. She'd always planned to get her ears pierced—she just hadn't planned to do it *today*. But somehow, having Angelica there made it more special.

Inside the jewelry store, a salesgirl helped her pick out a pair of tiny stud earrings.

 "You'll need to wear these for six weeks. Then you can wear anything you want," she explained as she led Mia to a chair in the corner.

She almost changed her mind when the woman took out something that looked like a staple gun. But just as Angelica promised, it didn't hurt much. Mia heard a pop and felt a hard pinch. A moment later, she was looking in the mirror at her new gold earrings.

It's amazing how something so small can make you look so different, she thought. The Mia who smiled back at her from the mirror seemed much more sophisticated than the old Mia.

"Everyone at home is going to be so surprised!" Angelica said.

Everyone? Mia suddenly thought of Kate and Lainey. She'd forgotten to tell them about her day with Angelica. Were they with the fairies now? Mia wondered.

Mia realized she still hadn't talked to her cousin about Pixie Hollow. The day had been so busy, there had never been the right moment. *I'll do it soon,* she promised herself.

They stopped at a diner and ordered fancy French dip sandwiches and Cokes with lemon slices. Angelica told funny stories about her friends at school. Mia laughed so hard that everyone at nearby tables turned to look—which made them both laugh harder.

Mia sipped her soda, feeling cool and grown-up, in a nice way. Everything about the day had been new and exciting—her earrings, the slice of lemon in her Coke, their adventure in the city. To Mia it felt as if she'd stepped through another portal. Only instead of Pixie Hollow, this portal led to a world of grown-up things.

Queen Clarion was wrong, Mia decided. *Just look at me. You* can *be grown-up and still believe in magic.* She was sure Angelica would think so, too.

"I need your help with something," Mia said.

"Sure. What is it?" her cousin said.

"Remember the fairies we told you about?"

"You mean, Gabby's fairies?" Angelica asked, nibbling a French fry.

"Yeah . . . well, not just Gabby's. They're our fairies, too—Kate's and Lainey's and mine. I mean, they're not *ours*. But we're the ones who found the hole. . . ."

Mia stumbled over her words. She took a breath and started over. "The fairies are our friends. They live in a place called Pixie Hollow. We can go there whenever we want, through a magical passage. But the fairies are in trouble—"

"I know," Angelica said, cutting her off.

"You do?" Mia asked, startled.

Angelica nodded. "Gabby already told me about it. The fairies are losing their magic, because not enough kids believe. Don't worry, I get it."

"You *do*?"

"Yeah," Angelica said. "You want me to play along. I think you're a sweet big sister for playing make-believe with Gabby."

Mia's heart sank. "But it's *not* make-believe.

That's what I'm trying to say!" Why was she having so much trouble making Angelica understand?

Angelica studied her for a moment. "Mia, I'm not saying this to be mean, okay? But you have to grow up sometime." She dipped another fry in her ketchup. "All this stuff about fairies and magic. I know we used to play games when we were little. But it's different now."

"What do you mean?" Mia asked.

Angelica sighed. "I mean, nobody believes in fairies anymore."

Chapter 12

The rainbow was gone. Kate could have kicked herself for losing it.

She called her mother, only to find out that all the toy-drive presents were gone. "The volunteers delivered the last ones today," Mrs. McCrady explained. "Is something the matter?"

"Lainey's dad accidentally gave away

the wrong box," Kate told her.

"Oh no. Was there something valuable in it?" her mother asked.

"Yes. Very," Kate said.

Her mother sighed. "Well, let me find the list of addresses. We'll probably have to check with a few different families. Hold on."

She heard her mom set down the phone. As she waited, Kate pictured herself knocking on strangers' doors. "Excuse me," she imagined herself saying. "I think you got something that belongs to me by mistake." She pictured a little boy or girl handing back the box—maybe the only present he or she would have that Christmas.

"Here it is," her mom said, when she picked up the phone again. "Can you tell me

what the box looked like? I'll start calling
the families—"

"Never mind," Kate said. "I was wrong. I
guess we don't need it back after all."

She hung up and went back to the kitchen
table where her friends were waiting.

"Well?" Lainey looked up expectantly.
"Did you find out where the rainbow went?"

Kate shook her head. She made a silent wish that whoever found it would share its magic.

Lainey sighed. "It's my fault. We should never have stopped to eat lunch."

"No, it's *my* fault," Kate said, feeling furious with herself all over again. "I shouldn't have left it sitting there."

Gabby looked up from her second cup of hot chocolate. "But can't Iridessa and Silvermist just make another one?" she asked.

Why didn't I think of that? Kate thought. She looked hopefully at the fairies. "Can you?"

"We could," said Silvermist. "We'll just need a crashing waterfall."

"And several blazing sunbeams," Iridessa added.

Kate's face fell. "But we don't have any of that. Can't you just do it with magic?"

"We have to start somewhere. Even *our* magic isn't strong enough to make a rainbow out of thin air," Iridessa explained.

"We'll have to go back to Pixie Hollow," Silvermist agreed.

"What will you tell Queen Clarion?" Kate asked anxiously as they walked back to the portal. She didn't want the queen to know she'd wasted the fairies' magic—she might not let the fairies come back to the mainland again.

"Don't worry. We'll think of something," Silvermist promised.

Kate watched the fairies fly through the door, into the lush green world of Pixie Hollow. She longed to follow them. But it was late in the day. She knew her parents would be expecting her.

"Come on, Gabby," she said. "I'll walk you home."

They said goodbye to Lainey. Outside, late-afternoon light was fading from the sky. As they started down the street, they saw Mia and Angelica returning from the bus stop. Mia had a pink shopping bag looped over one arm and was talking to her cousin.

Kate felt a sudden flare of anger. She stormed over to them. "Have a nice day?" she snapped. "Why didn't you tell us you were—" She stopped and stared. "What did you do to your ears?"

"Oh!" Mia reached up and touched the

small gold earrings. "I got them pierced today."

"They look cute, don't they?" Angelica said.

A feeling that had been boiling in Kate all afternoon suddenly spilled over. "Getting your ears pierced!" she exploded. "*That's* what was so important?"

"That's not what I—" Mia started to say.

But Kate was too worked up to listen. "*I'm* trying to help Pixie Hollow. *Lainey's* trying to help. Even Gabby's trying. You're the only one who isn't doing anything. All you care about is shopping and . . . and your *dumb* earrings!"

The look in Mia's eyes went flat. "You don't know what you're talking about. You don't know anything," she said. She turned toward her house. "Come on, Gabby. We're going inside."

Gabby looked from Kate to Mia. Mia shrugged and started off without her.

"I'll see you tomorrow," Gabby whispered to Kate. Then she turned and chased after her sister and cousin.

"What was that all about?" Kate heard Angelica say as they walked away.

"Nothing," came Mia's reply.

Kate stood frozen to her spot. She had the sudden, terrible feeling that she'd said everything wrong. But as Mia, Gabby, and Angelica turned up the steps to their house, she couldn't stop herself from shouting, "I hope you're happy. If their magic dies, it'll be your fault!"

Mia didn't even look back. Without a word, she went inside and closed the door.

Chapter 13

The next day, Lainey awoke with a feeling of excitement. She hurried to her window to look out at the toolshed, wondering what new magic it held for them today. The night had brought a fresh layer of snow. Beneath it, the shed looked huddled and secretive, giving nothing away.

After breakfast, Lainey dressed quickly

and hurried out to the backyard. She met Gabby coming around the side of the house by herself.

"Gabby, why are you alone?" Lainey asked.

"Papi said I could walk here by myself," Gabby told her proudly. "I told him it was really important. I wanted to see about the fairies."

"Where's Mia?" Lainey said.

"At home with Angelica. They're making bracelets," Gabby said.

"Bracelets! What for?"

Gabby shrugged. "For fun, I guess."

"But what about Pixie Hollow?" Lainey asked.

"She said she isn't coming," Gabby told her.

"Who isn't coming?" Kate asked, walking

up. She was pink-cheeked and breathless, as if she'd run the whole way there.

When she heard about Mia, Kate's face clouded. "Something is wrong," she said. "Mia isn't like this. Do you think she could have stopped believing?"

"How could she?" Lainey said, shocked. "We've been to Pixie Hollow so many times!"

"But yesterday she was acting really strange. Like she doesn't care about the fairies or Pixie Hollow," Kate said. "And Prilla said the Disbelief was contagious."

"Where could she have caught it?" Lainey asked.

"From Angelica," Kate said. "I've been thinking about it. Remember when we first told Angelica about Pixie Hollow? She called it make-believe."

"And then the portal closed," Lainey realized.

"Exactly," said Kate. "Never Land wouldn't let Angelica in because she doesn't believe."

"Does that mean Mia won't ever see fairies again?" Gabby asked.

As the girls stared at each other, considering this, they heard a *tap-tap-tap*. It was coming from inside the shed.

"The fairies! They must be back with more magic," Kate said, reaching for the door.

"Careful," Lainey warned her.

Kate flipped the latch and slowly eased the door open. But there were no butterflies and no rainbow, only a single fairy hovering in the doorway. It was Spring—a messenger-talent fairy.

"Queen Clarion asks you to come at once,"

Spring said. "It's urgent. We need your help. *Please.*"

The word "please" gave Lainey a jolt. Fairies almost never said please. The situation must have been desperate.

"What about Mia? Shouldn't we get her?" Lainey asked. If anything could cure their friend of the Disbelief, it would be seeing Pixie Hollow again.

"There's no time to wait," Spring said. With Spring flying in the lead, the girls hurried through the door in the wall and into Pixie Hollow.

Even as they stepped into the sunlight of Never Land, Lainey knew something was wrong. It was too quiet, and she suddenly realized why. The silvery sound of fairy laughter was missing.

Gabby ran ahead, then stopped with a wail. As Lainey and Kate came up behind her, they froze, too. Together the girls stared at the awful sight before them.

The Home Tree was bare. Its leafless branches looked stark and skeletal against the blue sky. The fairy windows that lined the branches were dark and empty.

Queen Clarion was waiting for them in

the pebble courtyard. She looked sad, and her wings were lowered in a defeated way. She clutched a petal handkerchief tightly in her hands. A small group of fairies were standing with her. Lainey saw Tinker Bell, Fawn, and Vidia among them.

"What happened?" Kate asked.

"The Home Tree is sick," Queen Clarion told her. "Our magic isn't strong enough to keep it alive."

The Home Tree was the heart of Pixie Hollow. If it died, where would the fairies live? Lainey wondered.

"But that's not all," Queen Clarion continued. "Prilla is hurt."

The girls gasped. "Was it on a blink?" asked Lainey.

The queen shook her head. "No. It happened here, in Pixie Hollow. A hawk caught her. It tore her wing—she was lucky to get away. She was exhausted from her blinks to the mainland. That's how the hawk managed to get so close."

"Will she be okay?" Gabby asked.

"I hope so," Queen Clarion replied. "She's with the healing-talent fairies now. But their magic is weak, too. Without Prilla to help us, I'm afraid the Disbelief will only get worse."

Lainey understood now why Queen Clarion had sent for them. The portal was the fairies' last chance.

"We have a plan," the queen said. She held out her hands, and Lainey saw that what she'd mistaken for a handkerchief was actually a note. On a white rose petal, the word "Believe" had been written in sparkling fairy dust.

"Right now we have fairies writing notes. I'm willing to send every fairy who can still fly to bring them to Clumsies in your world," the queen said. "Maybe if people see the notes, they'll believe again."

It was a good plan, Lainey thought. Even people who couldn't see fairies would be able to see the petals and their magical message. "What do you want us to do?" she asked.

"We'll need you to tell us where to go to reach the most Clumsies," Tinker Bell said.

"What about the Night Lights? Lots of people will be out then," Kate suggested.

"Good idea!" Lainey said. Every year on Christmas Eve, their neighborhood closed off some of the streets so people could stroll around looking at the holiday lights. Lots of families came. Lainey imagined hundreds of fairies flying over their heads, dropping their petal messages. It would be a glorious sight.

"It's really going to work!" Kate said, growing excited. "Let's get all the other fairies together."

The fairies were silent for a moment. Then Tink spoke up. "It will just be us. We're the only ones who can still fly."

"Just you?" Lainey looked at the small group. There couldn't have been more than a dozen fairies.

But that would have to be enough. Pixie Hollow was depending on them.

Chapter 14

The last bit of sunlight was fading from the sky. All up and down the street, colored lights on the houses and trees shone brightly in the gathering darkness. Kate stood with Lainey under a tall tree in front of Lainey's house. Groups of people passed them, filling the street with voices and laughter.

No one seemed to notice the fairies standing on the branches above the girls' heads. The fairies' soft yellow glows decorated the tree like Christmas lights.

"Is it time yet?" Lainey asked.

Kate glanced up at the fairies. They stood alert on their branches, sacks of flower-petal messages at their sides. She knew she should give them the signal to start. At this point, every minute counted in Pixie Hollow.

Still, Kate found herself saying, "Let's wait just a little longer. Maybe more people will come."

She looked up and down the street, hoping to spot Mia. Mia had stayed away all day, and Kate was worried that it was because of their fight. She didn't want Mia to miss the magic—Kate hoped the fairies could cure Mia's Disbelief, too.

A cold wind started to blow. Kate tightened her scarf and shivered.

"Kate," Lainey said, after a few more minutes had gone by, "I don't think we should wait any longer."

Just then, Kate saw Gabby running toward them. Her heart sank when she saw that Mia wasn't with her.

"Where's Mia?" she asked in dismay.

"She wanted to stay with Angelica," Gabby told her.

Kate saw Mia coming down the sidewalk, arm in arm with her cousin. Relief flooded through her. It wasn't too late for her friend to see the magic. "Mia! Over here!" Kate yelled, waving at her.

Mia stared at her for a moment. Then, to Kate's astonishment, she spun around and

began to hurry in the opposite direction, pulling Angelica with her.

What was going on? Kate wondered. She was about to run after her when there was a strong gust of wind.

Kate heard a cry above her. She looked up in time to see the fairies' petals go sailing into the air. For a moment, they swirled like snowflakes against the dark sky.

"Oh no!" Lainey wailed. "The messages!"

"What's happening to the fairies?" Gabby cried.

In the branches of the tree, the fairies' glows were starting to fade. They flickered like flames guttering in the wind.

"Their magic is dying!" Lainey said.

"Someone *do* something!" Gabby cried.

But there was nothing anyone could do. The girls watched helplessly as, one by one, the fairies' lights went out.

Chapter 15

Gabby clung to the tree trunk, staring up at the branches. But in the darkness she could no longer see the fairies. Were they even still there?

"Tink?" she called in a wobbly voice. "Fawn? Rosetta?" There was no reply.

Gabby did the only thing she could think of. She clapped her hands. "I believe," Gabby whispered. "I believe, I believe, I believe . . ."

People on the street turned to look at the little girl clapping up at an empty tree. Gabby didn't care. She took off her mittens and clapped harder. She clapped until her palms stung and her eyes were blurry with tears. But the tree remained dark.

At last, Lainey put a hand on her arm and told her to stop. An icy wind was blowing. Gabby shivered and put her freezing hands in her pockets. Could the fairies really be *gone*?

Then, suddenly, she heard a tiny jingle.

Gabby's heart leapt with hope. She searched the tree but didn't see even a faint glimmer. And yet . . . she could still hear fairies laughing.

Other people heard it, too. All along the

sidewalks, grown-ups and kids stopped to listen.

Mia came running over, with Angelica right behind her. "Do you hear that?" Mia asked her friends.

All of a sudden, Gabby knew what it was. "My bells!"

They were ringing out from all over, filling the air with magical sound. For several seconds, the whole street seemed to hold still in wonder.

Gabby held her breath, too. The sound of fairy laughter was growing, ringing out all over the street.

Gabby saw a flicker overhead, and another. Then, all at once, the branches of the tree blazed with light again. She could see the fairies twirling in the branches, their glows brighter than ever.

"It's working!" Gabby cried.

The fairies rose into the air. They looked like flames shining brightly against the night sky. Up and down the sidewalks, people gasped.

"Do you see that?"

"What are they?"

"Mommy, it's fairies!"

"It can't be . . . can it?"

"Ouch! Something pinched me!"

Lainey pointed at a blur of light streaking up to join the others. "There's Vidia!" she said, laughing.

"And look, there's Tink!" Gabby saw the tiny blond fairy darting through the air. She had Gabby's fairy bell in her hands and was waving it merrily. The sound of her laugh mingled with the ringing of the bell.

The crowd stood with their heads tipped back, watching the fairies dance through the night. The holiday lights on the houses were all but forgotten.

Gabby spied a familiar freckled fairy among the darting, dancing points of light. "There's Prilla!" she cried.

"But how did she get here?" Lainey asked. "Queen Clarion said she couldn't fly."

"She must have blinked here," Kate said. "That means she's all right!"

Prilla grinned and turned a cartwheel in midair. She flew to the other fairies, and they all joined hands. For a moment, they whirled through the air, a shining ring of light.

Then Prilla blinked—and in an instant the fairies disappeared.

For a moment the girls remained quiet, staring up at the sky where the fairies had been. Snippets of conversations drifted toward them.

". . . never seen anything like it . . ."

"If I didn't know better, I'd have said those really *were* fairies."

". . . magic, pure and simple."

"We did it," Gabby whispered.

"*You* did it," Kate said, scooping her up in a bear hug. "Who knew those bells would actually work!"

"Bells?" Mia asked. "What do you mean?"

When Gabby told her about the hidden bells, Mia hugged her, too. "Gabby, you're brilliant," she said. "I *knew* you guys would find a way to save Pixie Hollow."

The others looked at her in surprise. "You *did*?" Lainey asked.

"You sure could have fooled me," Kate said with a frown.

"We thought you caught the Disbelief, too," Gabby explained.

"Me?" Mia looked surprised. "Never! I'm sorry I stayed away. I was only trying to help," she explained. "Mami said I needed to spend time with Angelica—and I wanted to. But I was afraid if I brought her with us, the portal would close again."

"Why didn't you just tell us?" Kate asked.

Mia sighed. "Because I was afraid you wouldn't like Angelica anymore if I told you she didn't believe in fairies. And I thought if I could just make her believe again before you found out, then we could all go to Pixie Hollow together. Then you were so mean about me getting my ears pierced," she added. "Well, I was pretty mad."

"I shouldn't have called your earrings dumb," Kate said. "But I still can't believe you got your ears pierced. Did it hurt?"

"Only a little," Mia said. "Angelica convinced me."

"Where is she now?" Lainey asked.

They spotted Mia and Gabby's cousin standing a few feet away. She was still staring up at the place where the fairies had disappeared.

"Angelica, did you see the fairies?" Gabby asked.

Angelica blinked. When she turned, there was a faraway look in her eyes. "Gabby, you won't believe it. But I think I just saw my old fairy," she said.

Chapter 16

Christmas the next day was not very different from every Christmas that had come before. That is to say, it was lovely. There were many wonderful presents and lots of good food, and Mia, Gabby, Kate, and Lainey each had the cozy feeling of being in exactly the right place—home.

The only unusual occurrence that day

was the large rainbow arcing over the city—extraordinary, for the day had dawned clear and cold, without a cloud in sight. Throughout the day, it was much remarked on by children and grown-ups alike. No one could explain where the rainbow had come from, but it remained for most of the day, and gave the holiday an extra-special, magical feel.

The girls were so busy with their own families on Christmas that they didn't have time to discuss the fairies with each other. It wasn't until the day after Christmas that they learned the portal to Never Land was gone.

"Are you sure?" Mia asked. They were sitting in her kitchen. Angelica was upstairs in her room, packing up her things. She, Aunt Lara, and Uncle Jack were leaving that day.

Kate and Lainey had come to see them off.

"I'm sure," Lainey said. "I went out to the shed this morning. The door in the wall is gone."

Kate sighed. "It must have moved again. I suppose it will turn up somewhere else."

Lainey fiddled with the friendship bracelet she was wearing. Mia had given one to each of them. "You think the fairies are all right, though, don't you?" she whispered.

The girls looked at each other, considering. "Yeah," Kate said. "I do."

"Me too," said Gabby.

"So do I," Mia agreed. "I don't know how I know. I just do." Deep in her heart, she felt sure all was well in Pixie Hollow. "I wish Angelica could have seen it, though. I know she would have loved it."

"There's always next year," Lainey said.

Mia nodded, though she was thinking that a lot could change in a year. *But I'll never stop believing in fairies,* she thought. That was one thing she knew would never change.

Uncle Jack came downstairs with the suitcases then. It was time to say good-bye. Aunt

Lara was misty-eyed as she hugged Mia and Gabby. "I can't believe it will be a whole year till I see you next," she said. "You girls will be all grown up by then!"

"I hope not!" Gabby exclaimed.

Mia gave Angelica an extra-long hug. "Thanks for my new earrings," she said. For Christmas, Angelica had given her a pair of earrings like the ones they'd seen in the bead shop. "I'll send you a picture as soon as I can wear them."

"Thanks for the book of fairy tales," Angelica said. "I'm going to read it on the drive home." She leaned closer to Mia and whispered, "Sometimes I do believe in fairies. Just a little bit."

Mia smiled. "I know," she whispered back.

After more hugs and a few tears, Angelica

and her parents got in their car and drove away. Mia, Gabby, and their friends stood on the front steps waving until they were out of sight.

Chapter 17

"Look what came in the mail," Kate said.

It was the last day of winter break, and the four friends were in Mia and Gabby's backyard. Gabby was trying to make a snowman out of the melting snow, and the other girls were helping. It was an unusually warm winter day, and they'd come outside to enjoy the sunshine.

Kate pulled an envelope out of her coat pocket. Inside was a letter written in crayon.

Dear Mr. or Mrs.,

Thank you for the byutifull rainbow. It was the best present. I think fairys must have made it because it was so magik.

Love, Naomi

"Maybe losing the rainbow wasn't such a bad thing after all," Lainey said.

"Don't you think it's weird that we haven't heard anything from Never Land, though?"

Kate said. It had been more than a week since they'd seen the fairies blinking away in the night sky. They'd checked the toolshed every day, but the portal still hadn't reappeared. The girls missed their visits to Pixie Hollow. "You'd think *they* might send a thank-you note, at least, after all we did to help," she added sourly.

"Maybe they're still busy getting their magic back to normal," Mia said. "Anyway, it's not the fairies' fault the hole closed. They always said it was just Never Land's magic."

Kate gave the soccer ball a hard kick so it bounced off the fence. "Well, phooey on Never Land, then. Why open a portal if you're only going to close it?"

"Maybe the portal was there

just so we could help the fairies when they needed us," Lainey said.

"I don't believe that," Mia said. "I don't believe we'll never go back again."

"Maybe some other kids found the portal somewhere else and they're visiting Pixie Hollow right now," Kate grouched. Everyone was quiet for a moment.

Gabby looked up from the large snowball she was pushing. "Maybe it's already here," she said. "Maybe it's just waiting for *us* to find it again."

The girls looked around. There was a fresh, earthy smell in the air. Even though it was only January, they could sense spring just around the corner.

"What's that on your shoulder, Gabby?" Kate asked.

As Gabby twisted to look, something yellow fluttered into the air. "A butterfly!"

The girls looked at each other. It wasn't spring that was just around the corner. It was Never Land!

"Quick!" said Kate. "Follow that butterfly!"

The butterfly flew high into the sky, then disappeared over the fence.

"It's gone!" Lainey cried.

But even as she said it, the girls could feel a warm breeze on their faces, blowing through the slats of the fence. When they touched it, they discovered that the boards were loose again—just like they had been when the magic first started.

"Come on!" Kate cried, pushing against a loose board. Through the hole, she could hear the unmistakable jingle of fairy laughter. Pixie Hollow was just ahead. They were going back to Never Land!

Something is happening,
Lainey thought.
As she reached for the latch
on the toolshed,
her fingertips tingled
with excitement.

The bell jingled in the wind.
Gabby smiled.
It was the sound of a fairy,
the sound of Pixie Hollow.

Kate stuck her hand into the shed.
Her fingers passed right through
the light and lit up blue.
The rainbow rippled like water
where she touched it.
"Wow," she gasped.

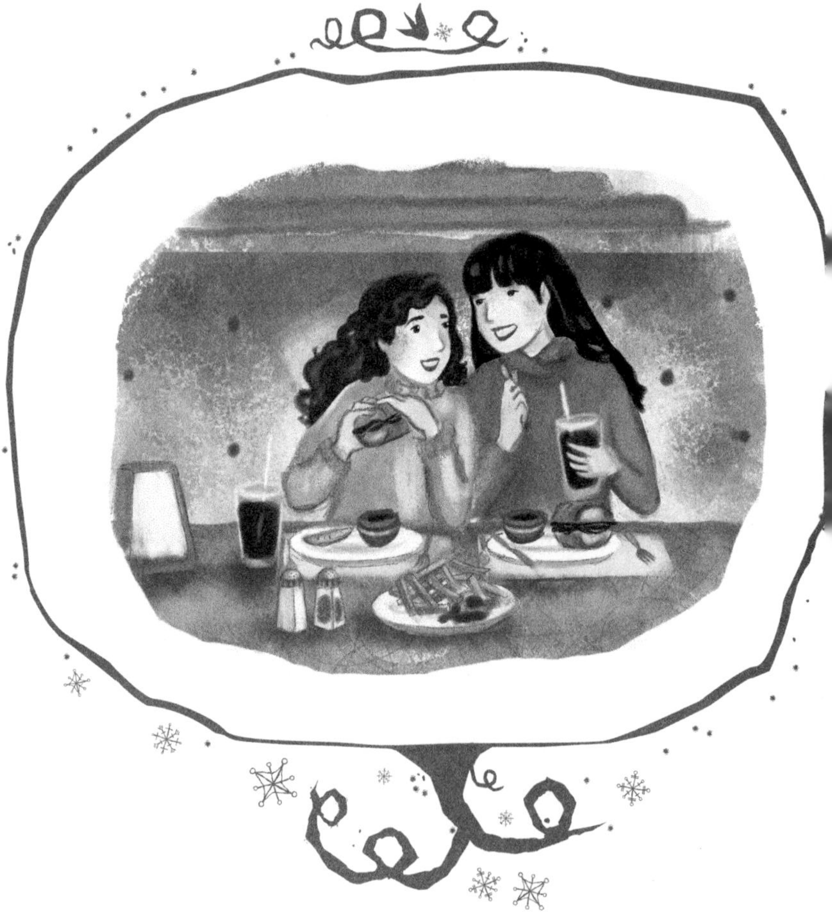

Everything about the day had been
new and exciting—her earrings,
the slice of lemon in her coke,
their adventure in the city.
To Mia it felt as if she'd stepped
through another portal.

The fairies rose into the air. They looked like flames shining brightly against the night sky. Up and down the sidewalks, people gasped.